811
Ash   Ashbery
        A wave

14.95

· A WAVE ·

ALSO BY JOHN ASHBERY

POETRY

SOME TREES

THE TENNIS COURT OATH

RIVERS AND MOUNTAINS

THE DOUBLE DREAM OF SPRING

THREE POEMS

THE VERMONT NOTEBOOK

SELF-PORTRAIT IN A CONVEX MIRROR

HOUSEBOAT DAYS

AS WE KNOW

SHADOW TRAIN

FICTION

A NEST OF NINNIES
(WITH JAMES SCHUYLER)

PLAYS

THREE PLAYS

·A WAVE·

POEMS BY
JOHN ASHBERY

THE VIKING PRESS
NEW YORK

LIBRARY OF CONGRESS CATALOGING IN PUBLICATION DATA
Ashbery, John.
  A wave.
  I. Title.
PS3501.S475W3   1984   811'.54   83-40217
ISBN 0-670-75176-6

Acknowledgment is made to the following publications, in which some of the poems in this book appeared originally: *American Poetry Review:* "A Wave"; *Conjunctions:* "When the Sun Went Down," "A Fly," "I See, Said the Blind Man, as He Put Down His Hammer and Saw," "Destiny Waltz," "Problems," and "They Like"; *Grand Street:* "But What Is the Reader to Make of This?" "Purists Will Object," and "Darlene's Hospital"; *Mothers of Mud:* "Edition Peters, Leipzig"; *New York Arts Journal:* "Cups with Broken Handles" and "The Path to the White Moon"; *New York Review of Books:* "Landscape (After Baudelaire)" and "More Pleasant Adventures"; *The New Yorker:* "At North Farm," "Down by the Station Early in the Morning," "Proust's Questionnaire," "The Ongoing Story," and "Never Seek to Tell Thy Love"; *Paris Review:* "Rain Moving In"; *Rolling Stone:* "Staffage"; *Sulphur:* "37 Haiku," "Haibun (1–6)," and "So Many Lives"; *Times Literary Supplement:* "Just Walking Around," "The Songs We Know Best," "Thank You for Not Cooperating," and "Trefoil"; *Vanity Fair:* "Around the Rough and Rugged Rocks the Ragged Rascal Rudley Ran"; *Virginia Quarterly Review:* "The Lonedale Operator."

"Variation on a Noel," "The Songs We Know Best," "The Lonedale Operator," and "Whatever It Is, Wherever You Are" appear in *Apparitions,* a limited edition anthology published by Lord John Press. "Description of a Masque" appears in *Contemporary American Fiction,* an anthology published by Sun & Moon Press.

Grateful acknowledgment is made to the following for permission to reprint copyrighted material:
EMI Music Company: Portions of lyrics from the song "Sentimental Journey," by Les Brown and Benjamin Homer. Used by permission of Morley Music, c/o Colgems EMI Music, Inc., Hollywood, California. All rights reserved.
Oxford University Press, England: A selection from "When We Dead Awaken," by Henrik Isben, from *The Oxford Ibsen,* Vol. VIII.

· CONTENTS ·

AT NORTH FARM   1

RAIN MOVING IN   2

THE SONGS WE KNOW BEST   3

WHEN THE SUN WENT DOWN   6

LANDSCAPE (AFTER BAUDELAIRE)   7

JUST WALKING AROUND   8

A FLY   9

THE ONGOING STORY   11

THANK YOU FOR NOT COOPERATING   12

BUT WHAT IS THE READER TO MAKE OF THIS?   13

DOWN BY THE STATION, EARLY IN THE MORNING   14

AROUND THE ROUGH AND RUGGED ROCKS THE
    RAGGED RASCAL RUDELY RAN   15

MORE PLEASANT ADVENTURES   16

PURISTS WILL OBJECT   17

DESCRIPTION OF A MASQUE   18

THE PATH TO THE WHITE MOON   31

DITTO, KIDDO   33

INTRODUCTION   34

I SEE, SAID THE BLIND MAN, AS HE PUT DOWN HIS HAMMER AND SAW   35

EDITION PETERS, LEIPZIG   36

37 HAIKU   37

HAIBUN   39

HAIBUN 2	40
HAIBUN 3	41
HAIBUN 4	42
HAIBUN 5	43
HAIBUN 6	44
VARIATION ON A NOEL	45
STAFFAGE	47
THE LONEDALE OPERATOR	48
PROUST'S QUESTIONNAIRE	50
CUPS WITH BROKEN HANDLES	51
JUST SOMEONE YOU SAY HI TO	52
THEY LIKE	53
SO MANY LIVES	54
NEVER SEEK TO TELL THY LOVE	56
DARLENE'S HOSPITAL	57
DESTINY WALTZ	60
TRY ME! I'M DIFFERENT!	61
ONE OF THE MOST EXTRAORDINARY THINGS IN LIFE	62
WHATEVER IT IS, WHEREVER YOU ARE	63
TREFOIL	66
PROBLEMS	67
A WAVE	68

· AT NORTH FARM ·

Somewhere someone is traveling furiously toward you,
At incredible speed, traveling day and night,
Through blizzards and desert heat, across torrents, through narrow passes.
But will he know where to find you,
Recognize you when he sees you,
Give you the thing he has for you?

Hardly anything grows here,
Yet the granaries are bursting with meal,
The sacks of meal piled to the rafters.
The streams run with sweetness, fattening fish;
Birds darken the sky. Is it enough
That the dish of milk is set out at night,
That we think of him sometimes,
Sometimes and always, with mixed feelings?

· RAIN MOVING IN ·

The blackboard is erased in the attic
And the wind turns up the light of the stars,
Sinewy now. Someone will find out, someone will know.
And if somewhere on this great planet
The truth is discovered, a patch of it, dried, glazed by the sun,
It will just hang on, in its own infamy, humility. No one
Will be better for it, but things can't get any worse.
Just keep playing, mastering as you do the step
Into disorder this one meant. Don't you see
It's all we can do? Meanwhile, great fires
Arise, as of haystacks aflame. The dial has been set
And that's ominous, but all your graciousness in living
Conspires with it, now that this is our home:
A place to be from, and have people ask about.

· THE SONGS WE KNOW BEST ·

Just like a shadow in an empty room
Like a breeze that's pointed from beyond the tomb
Just like a project of which no one tells—
Or didja really think that I was somebody else?

Your clothes and pantlegs lookin' out of shape
Shape of the body over which they drape
Body which has acted in so many scenes
But didja ever think of what that body means?

It is an organ and a vice to some
A necessary evil which we all must shun
To others an abstraction and a piece of meat
But when you're looking out you're in the driver's seat!

No man cares little about fleshly things
They fill him with a silence that spreads in rings
We wish to know more but we are never sated
No wonder some folks think the flesh is overrated!

The things we know now all got learned in school
Try to learn a new thing and you break the rule
Our knowledge isn't much it's just a small amount
But you feel it quick inside you when you're down for the count

You look at me and frown like I was out of place
I guess I never did much for the human race
Just hatched some schemes on paper that looked good at first
Sat around and watched until the bubble burst

And now you're lookin' good all up and down the line
Except for one thing you still have in mind
It's always there though often with a different face
It's the worm inside the jumping bean that makes it race

Too often when you thought you'd be showered with confetti
What they flung at you was a plate of hot spaghetti
You've put your fancy clothes and flashy gems in hock
Yet you pause before your father's door afraid to knock

Once you knew the truth it tried to set you free
And still you stood transfixed just like an apple tree
The truth it came and went and left you in the lurch
And now you think you see it from your lofty perch

The others come and go they're just a dime a dozen
You react to them no more than to a distant cousin
Only a few people can touch your heart
And they too it seems have all gotten a false start

In twilight the city with its hills shines serene
And lets you make of it more than anything could mean
It's the same city by day that seems so crude and calm
You'll have to get to know it not just pump its arm

Even when that bugle sounded loud and clear
You knew it put an end to all your fear
To all that lying and the senseless mistakes
And now you've got it right and you know what it takes

Someday I'll look you up when we're both old and gray
And talk about those times we had so far away
How much it mattered then and how it matters still
Only things look so different when you've got a will

It's true that out of this misunderstanding could end
And men would greet each other like they'd found a friend
With lots of friends around there's no one to entice
And don't you think seduction isn't very nice?

It carries in this room against the painted wall
And hangs in folds of curtains when it's not there at all
It's woven in the flowers of the patterned spread
And lies and knows not what it thinks upon the bed

I wish to come to know you get to know you all
Let your belief in me and me in you stand tall
Just like a project of which no one tells—
Or do ya still think that I'm somebody else?

· WHEN THE SUN WENT DOWN ·

To have been loved once by someone—surely
There is a permanent good in that,
Even if we don't know all the circumstances
Or it happened too long ago to make any difference.
Like almost too much sunlight or an abundance of sweet-sticky,
Caramelized things—who can tell you it's wrong?
Which of the others on your team could darken the passive
Melody that runs on, that has been running since the world began?

Yet, to be strapped to one's mindset, which seems
As enormous as a plain, to have to be told
That its horizons are comically confining,
And all the sorrow wells from there, like the slanting
Plume of a waterspout: doesn't it supplant knowledge
Of the different forms of love, reducing them
To a white indifferent prism, a roofless love standing open
To the elements? And some see in this a paradigm of how it rises
Slowly to the indifferent heavens, all that pale glamour?

The refrain is desultory as birdsong; it seeps unrecognizably
Into the familiar structures that lead out from here
To the still familiar peripheries and less sure notions:
It already had its way. In time for evening relaxation.
There are times when music steals a march on us,
Is suddenly perplexingly nearer, flowing in my wrist;
Is the true and dirty words you whisper nightly
As the book closes like a collapsing sheet, a blur
Of all kinds of connotations ripped from the hour and tossed
Like jewels down a well; the answer, also,
To the question that was on my mind but that I've forgotten,
Except in the way certain things, certain nights, come together.

· LANDSCAPE ·
(After Baudelaire)

I want a bedroom near the sky, an astrologer's cave
Where I can fashion eclogues that are chaste and grave.
Dreaming, I'll hear the wind in the steeples close by
Sweep the solemn hymns away. I'll spy
On factories from my attic window, resting my chin
In both hands, drinking in the songs, the din.
I'll see chimneys and steeples, those masts of the city,
And the huge sky that makes us dream of eternity.

How sweet to watch the birth of the star in the still-blue
Sky, through mist; the lamp burning anew
At the window; rivers of coal climbing the firmament
And the moon pouring out its pale enchantment.
I'll see the spring, the summer and the fall
And when winter casts its monotonous pall
Of snow, I'll draw the blinds and curtains tight
And build my magic palaces in the night;
Then dream of gardens, of bluish horizons,
Of jets of water weeping in alabaster basins,
Of kisses, of birds singing at dawn and at nightfall,
Of all that's most childish in our pastoral.
When the storm rattles my windowpane
I'll stay hunched at my desk, it will roar in vain
For I'll have plunged deep inside the thrill
Of conjuring spring with the force of my will,
Coaxing the sun from my heart, and building here
Out of my fiery thoughts, a tepid atmosphere.

· JUST WALKING AROUND ·

What name do I have for you?
Certainly there is no name for you
In the sense that the stars have names
That somehow fit them. Just walking around,

An object of curiosity to some,
But you are too preoccupied
By the secret smudge in the back of your soul
To say much, and wander around,

Smiling to yourself and others.
It gets to be kind of lonely
But at the same time off-putting,
Counterproductive, as you realize once again

That the longest way is the most efficient way,
The one that looped among islands, and
You always seemed to be traveling in a circle.
And now that the end is near

The segments of the trip swing open like an orange.
There is light in there, and mystery and food.
Come see it. Come not for me but it.
But if I am still there, grant that we may see each other.

· A FLY ·

And still I automatically look to that place on the wall—
The timing is right, but off—
The approval soured—
That's what comes of age but not aging,
The marbles all snapped into the side pockets,
The stance for today we know full well is
Yesterday's delivery and ripe prediction—
The way not to hold in when circling,
As a delighted draughtsman sits down to his board.

Reasons, reasons for this:
The enthusiast mopping through his hair again
As he squats on the toilet and catches one eye in the mirror
(Guys it has come through all right
For once as delivered it's all here and me with time on my hands
For once, with writing to spare, and how many
Times have there been words to waste,
That you had to spend or else take big losses
In the car after an early dinner the endless
Light streaking out of the windshield
A breakthrough
I guess but don't just now take into account,
Don't look at the time) and time
Comes looking for you, out of Pennsylvania and New Jersey
It doesn't travel well
Colors his hair beige
Paints the straw walls gilds the mirror

The thing is that this is places in the world,
Freedom from rent,
Sundries, food, a dictionary to keep you company
Enviously
But is also the day we all got together
That the treaty was signed

And it all eased off into the big afternoon off the coast
Slid shoulders into the groundswell removed its boots
That we may live now with some
Curiosity and hope
Like pools that soon become part of the tide

I could say it's the happiest period of my life.
It hasn't got much competition! Yesterday
It seemed a flatness, hotness. As though it barely stood out
From the rocks of all the years before. Today it sheds
That old name, without assuming any new one. I think it's still there.

It was as though I'd been left with the empty street
A few seconds after the bus pulled out. A dollop of afternoon wind.
Others tell you to take your attention off it
For awhile, refocus the picture. Plan to entertain,
To get out. (Do people really talk that way?)

We could pretend that all that isn't there never existed anyway.
The great ideas? What good are they if they're misplaced,
In the wrong order, if you can't remember one
At the moment you're so to speak mounting the guillotine
Like Sydney Carton, and can't think of anything to say?
Or is this precisely material covered in a course
Called Background of the Great Ideas, and therefore it isn't necessary
To say anything or even know anything? The breath of the moment
Is breathed, we fall and still feel better. The phone rings,

It's a wrong number, and your heart is lighter,
Not having to be faced with the same boring choices again
Which doesn't undermine a feeling for people in general and
Especially in particular: you,
In your deliberate distinctness, whom I love and gladly
Agree to walk blindly into the night with,
Your realness is real to me though I would never take any of it
Just to see how it grows. A knowledge that people live close by is,
I think, enough. And even if only first names are ever exchanged
The people who own them seem rock-true and marvelously self-sufficient.

· THANK YOU FOR
NOT COOPERATING ·

Down in the street there are ice-cream parlors to go to
And the pavement is a nice, bluish slate-gray. People laugh a lot.
Here you can see the stars. Two lovers are singing
Separately, from the same rooftop: "*Leave your change behind,*
Leave your clothes, and go. It is time now.
It was time before too, but now it is really time.
You will never have enjoyed storms so much
As on these hot sticky evenings that are more like August
Than September. Stay. A fake wind wills you to go
And out there on the stormy river witness buses bound for Connecticut,
And tree-business, and all that we think about when we stop thinking.
The weather is perfect, the season unclear. Weep for your going
But also expect to meet me in the near future, when I shall disclose
New further adventures, and that you shall continue to think of me."

The wind dropped, and the lovers
Sang no more, communicating each to each in the tedium
Of self-expression, and the shore curled up and became liquid
And so the celebrated lament began. And how shall we, people
All unused to each other and to our own business, explain
It to the shore if it is given to us
To circulate there "in the near future" the why of our coming
And why we were never here before? The counterproposals
Of the guest-stranger impede our construing of ourselves as
Person-objects, the ones we knew would get here
Somehow, but we can remember as easily as the day we were born
The maggots we passed on the way and how the day bled
And the night too on hearing us, though we spoke only our childish
Ideas and never tried to impress anybody even when somewhat older.

· BUT WHAT IS THE READER
TO MAKE OF THIS? ·

A lake of pain, an absence
Leading to a flowering sea? Give it a quarter-turn
And watch the centuries begin to collapse
Through each other, like floors in a burning building,
Until we get to this afternoon:

Those delicious few words spread around like jam
Don't matter, nor does the shadow.
We have lived blasphemously in history
And nothing has hurt us or can.
But beware of the monstrous tenderness, for out of it
The same blunt archives loom. Facts seize hold of the web
And leave it ash. Still, it is the personal,
Interior life that gives us something to think about.
The rest is only drama.

Meanwhile the combinations of every extendable circumstance
In our lives continue to blow against it like new leaves
At the edge of a forest a battle rages in and out of
For a whole day. It's not the background, we're the background,
On the outside looking out. The surprises history has
For us are nothing compared to the shock we get
From each other, though time still wears
The colors of meanness and melancholy, and the general life
Is still many sizes too big, yet
Has style, woven of things that never happened
With those that did, so that a mood survives
Where life and death never could. Make it sweet again!

· DOWN BY THE STATION,
EARLY IN THE MORNING ·

It all wears out. I keep telling myself this, but
I can never believe me, though others do. Even things do.
And the things they do. Like the rasp of silk, or a certain
Glottal stop in your voice as you are telling me how you
Didn't have time to brush your teeth but gargled with Listerine
Instead. Each is a base one might wish to touch once more

Before dying. There's the moment years ago in the station in Venice,
The dark rainy afternoon in fourth grade, and the shoes then,
Made of a dull crinkled brown leather that no longer exists.
And nothing does, until you name it, remembering, and even then
It may not have existed, or existed only as a result
Of the perceptual dysfunction you've been carrying around for years.
The result is magic, then terror, then pity at the emptiness,
Then air gradually bathing and filling the emptiness as it leaks,
Emoting all over something that is probably mere reportage
But nevertheless likes being emoted on. And so each day
Culminates in merriment as well as a deep shock like an electric one,

As the wrecking ball bursts through the wall with the bookshelves
Scattering the works of famous authors as well as those
Of more obscure ones, and books with no author, letting in
Space, and an extraneous babble from the street
Confirming the new value the hollow core has again, the light
From the lighthouse that protects as it pushes us away.

· AROUND THE ROUGH AND RUGGED ROCKS THE RAGGED RASCAL RUDELY RAN ·

I think a lot about it,
Think quite a lot about it—
The omnipresent possibility of being interrupted
While what I stand for is still almost a bare canvas:
A few traceries, that may be fibers, perhaps
Not even these but shadows, hallucinations. . . .

And it is well then to recall
That this track is the outer rim of a flat crust,
Dimensionless, except for its poor, parched surface,
The face one raises to God,
Not the rich dark composite
We keep to ourselves,
Carpentered together any old way,
Coffee from an old tin can, a belch of daylight,
People leaving the beach.
If I could write it
And also write about it—
The interruption—
Rudeness on the face of it, but who
Knows anything about our behavior?

Forget what it is you're coming out of,
Always into something like a landscape
Where no one has ever walked
Because they're too busy.
Excitedly you open your rhyming dictionary.
It has begun to snow.

The first year was like icing.
Then the cake started to show through.
Which was fine, too, except you forget the direction you're taking.
Suddenly you are interested in some new thing
And can't tell how you got here. Then there is confusion
Even out of happiness, like a smoke—
The words get heavy, some topple over, you break others.
And outlines disappear once again.

Heck, it's anybody's story,
A sentimental journey—"gonna take a sentimental journey,"
And we do, but you wake up under the table of a dream:
You are that dream, and it is the seventh layer of you.
We haven't moved an inch, and everything has changed.
We are somewhere near a tennis court at night.
We get lost in life, but life knows where we are.
We can always be found with our associates.
Haven't you always wanted to curl up like a dog and go to sleep like a dog?

In the rash of partings and dyings (the new twist),
There's also room for breaking out of living.
Whatever happens will be quite ingenious.
No acre but will resume being disputed now,
And paintings are one thing we never seem to run out of.

· PURISTS WILL OBJECT ·

We have the looks you want:
The gonzo (musculature seemingly wired to the stars);
Colors like lead, khaki and pomegranate; things you
Put in your hair, with the whole panoply of the past:
Landscape embroidery, complete sets of this and that.
It's bankruptcy, the human haul,
The shining, bulging nets lifted out of the sea, and always a few refugees
Dropping back into the no-longer-mirthful kingdom
On the day someone sells an old house
And someone else begins to add on to his: all
In the interests of this pornographic masterpiece,
Variegated, polluted skyscraper to which all gazes are drawn,
Pleasure we cannot and will not escape.

It seems we were going home.
The smell of blossoming privet blanketed the narrow avenue.
The traffic lights were green and aqueous.
So this is the subterranean life.
If it can't be conjugated onto us, what good is it?
What need for purists when the demotic is built to last,
To outlast us, and no dialect hears us?

· DESCRIPTION OF A MASQUE ·

The persimmon velvet curtain rose swiftly to reveal a space of uncertain dimensions and perspective. At the lower left was a grotto, the cave of Mania, goddess of confusion. Larches, alders and Douglas fir were planted so thickly around the entrance that one could scarcely make it out. In the dooryard a hyena chained to a pole slunk back and forth, back and forth, continually measuring the length of its chain, emitting the well-known laughing sound all the while, except at intervals when what appeared to be fragments of speech would issue from its maw. It was difficult to hear the words, let alone understand them, though now and then a phrase like "Up your arse!" or "Turn the rascals out!" could be distinguished for a moment, before subsiding into a confused chatter. Close by the entrance to the grotto was a metal shoescraper in the form of a hyena, and very like this particular one, whose fur was a grayish-white faintly tinged with pink, and scattered over with foul, liver-colored spots. On the other side of the dooryard opposite the hyena's pole was a graceful statue of Mercury on a low, gilded pedestal, facing out toward the audience with an expression of delighted surprise on his face. The statue seemed to be made of lead or some other dull metal, painted an off-white which had begun to flake in places, revealing the metal beneath which was of almost the same color. As yet there was no sign of the invisible proprietress of the grotto.

A little to the right and about eight feet above this scene, another seemed to hover in mid-air. It suggested the interior of an English pub, as it might be imitated in Paris. Behind the bar, opposite the spectators in the audience, was a mural adapted from a Tenniel illustration for *Through the Looking Glass*—the famous one in which a fish in a footman's livery holds out a large envelope to a frog footman who has just emerged onto the front stoop of a small house, while in the background, partially concealed by the trunk of a tree, Alice lurks, an expression of amusement on her face. Time and the fumes of a public house had darkened the colors almost to a rich mahogany glow, and if one had not known the illustration it would have been difficult to make out some of the details.

Seven actors and actresses, representing seven nursery-rhyme char-

acters, populated the scene. Behind the bar the bald barman, Georgie
Porgie, stood motionless, gazing out at the audience. In front and a little
to his left, lounging on a tall stool, was Little Jack Horner, in fact quite a
tall and roguish-looking young man wearing a trench coat and expensive
blue jeans; he had placed his camera on the bar near him. He too faced
out toward the audience. In front of him, his back to the audience, Little
Boy Blue partially knelt before him, apparently performing an act of fel-
latio on him. Boy Blue was entirely clothed in blue denim, of an ordinary kind.

To their left, Simple Simon and the Pie Man stood facing each other
in profile. The Pie Man's gaze was directed toward the male couple at the
center of the bar; at the same time he continually offered and withdrew a
pie coveted by Simon, whose attention was divided between the pie and
the scene behind him, at which he kept glancing over his shoulder, immediately turning back toward the pie as the Pie Man withdrew it,
Simon all the time pretending to fumble in his pocket for a penny. The
Pie Man was dressed like a French baker's apprentice, in a white blouse
and blue-and-white checked pants; he appeared to be about twenty-eight
years of age. Simon was about the same age, but he was wearing a Buster
Brown outfit, with a wide-brimmed hat, dark blue blazer and short
pants, and a large red bow tie.

At the opposite end of the bar sat two young women, their backs to
the audience, apparently engaged in conversation. The first, Polly
Flinders, was wearing a strapless dress of ash-colored chiffon with a narrow silver belt. She sat closest to Jack Horner and Boy Blue, but paid no
attention to them and turned frequently toward her companion, at the
same time puffing on a cigarette in a shiny black cigarette holder and
sipping a martini straight up with an olive. Daffy Down Dilly, the other
young woman, had long straight blond hair which had obviously been
brushed excessively so that it gleamed when it caught the light; it was
several shades of blond in easily distinguishable streaks. She wore a long
emerald- green velvet gown cut very low in back, and held up by
glittering rhinestone straps; her yellow lace-edged petticoat hung down
about an inch and a half below the hem of her gown. She did not smoke

but from time to time sipped through a straw on a whiskey sour, also straight up. Although she frequently faced in the direction of the other characters when she turned toward Polly, she too paid them no mind.

After a few moments Jack seemed to grow weary of Boy Blue's attentions and gave him a brisk shove which sent him sprawling on the floor, where he walked about on all fours barking like a dog for several minutes, causing the hyena in the bottom left tableau to stop its own prowling and fall silent except for an occasional whimper, as though wondering where the barking was coming from. Soon Boy Blue curled up in front of the bar and pretended to fall asleep, resting his head on the brass rail, and the hyena continued as before. Jack rearranged his clothing and turned toward the barman, who handed him another drink. At this point the statue of Mercury stepped from its pedestal and seemed to float upward into the bar scene, landing on tiptoe between Jack and Simple Simon. After a deep bow in the direction of the ladies, who ignored him, he turned to face the audience and delivered the following short speech.

"My fellow prisoners, we have no idea how long each of us has been in this town and how long each of us intends to stay, although I have reason to believe that the lady in green over there is a fairly recent arrival. My point, however, is this. Instead of loitering this way, we should all become part of a collective movement, get involved with each other and with our contemporaries on as many levels as possible. No one will disagree that there is much to be gained from contact with one another, and I, as a god, feel it even more keenly than you do. My understanding, though universal, lacks the personal touch and the local color which would make it meaningful to me."

These words seemed to produce an uneasiness among the other patrons of the bar. Even Little Boy Blue stopped pretending to be asleep and glanced warily at the newcomer. The two girls had left off conversing. After a few moments Daffy got down off her bar stool and walked over to Mercury. Opening a green brocade pocketbook, she pulled out a small revolver and shot him in the chest. The bullet passed through him without harming him and imbedded itself in the fish in the mural behind the bar, causing it to lurch forward regurgitating blood and drop the envelope, which produced a loud report and a flash like a magnesium flare that illuminated an expression of anger and fear on Alice's face, as she hastily clapped her hands over her ears. Then the whole stage was plunged in darkness, the last thing remaining visible being the apparently permanent smile on Mercury's face—still astonished and delighted, and bearing no trace of malice.

Little by little the darkness began to dissipate, and a forest scene similar to that in the mural was revealed. It had moved forward to fill the space formerly occupied by the bar and its customers, and was much neater and tidier than the forest in the mural had been. The trees were more or less the same size and shape, and planted equidistant from each other. There was no forest undergrowth, no dead leaves or rotting tree trunks on the ground; the grass under the trees was as green and well kept as that of a lawn. This was because the scene represented a dream of Mania (whose grotto was still visible in the lower left-hand corner of the stage), and, since she was the goddess of confusion, her dream revealed no trace of confusion, or at any rate presented a confusing absence of confusion. On a white banner threaded through some of the branches of the trees in the foreground the sentence "It's an Ongoing Thing" was printed in scarlet letters. To the left, toward the rear of the scene, Alice appeared to be asleep at the base of a tree trunk, with a pig dressed in baby clothes asleep in her lap. An invisible orchestra in the pit intoned the "March" from Grieg's *Sigurd Jorsalfar*. A group of hobos who had previously been hidden behind the trees moved to the center of the stage and began to perform a slow-moving ballet to the music. Each was dressed identically in baggy black-and-white checked trousers held up by white suspenders fastened with red buttons, a crumpled black swallowtail coat, red flannel undershirt, brown derby hat and white gloves with black stripes outlining the contours of the wrist bones, and each held in his right hand an extinguished cigar butt with a fat gray puffy ash affixed to it. Moving delicately on point, the group formed an ever-narrowing semicircle around Alice and the sleeping pig, when a sudden snort from the latter startled them and each disappeared behind a tree. At this moment Mania emerged from her grotto dressed in a gown of sapphire-blue tulle studded with blue sequins, cradling a sheaf of white gladioli in the crook of one arm and with her other hand holding aloft a wand with a gilt cardboard star at its tip. Only her curiously unkempt hair marred the somewhat dated elegance of her toilette. Deftly detaching the hyena's chain from its post, she allowed the beast to lead her upward to the forest scene where the hobos had each begun to peek out from behind his tree trunk. Like the Wilis in *Giselle*, they appeared mesmerized by the apparition of the goddess, swaying to the movement of her star-tipped wand as she waved it, describing wide arcs around herself. None dared draw too close, however, for if they did so the snarling, slavering hyena would lurch forward, straining at its chain. At length she let her wand droop toward the ground, and after gazing pensively downward for some moments she raised her head and, tossing back her matted curls, spoke thus:

"My sister *Hecat*, who sometimes accompanies me on midnight rides to nameless and indescribable places, warned me of this dell, seemingly laid out for the Sunday strolls of civil servants, but in reality the haunt of drifters and retarded children. *You*," she cried, shaking her wand at the corps de ballet of hobos, who stumbled and fell over each other in their frantic attempt to get away from her, " you who oppress even my dreams, where a perverse order should reign but where I find instead traces of the lunacy that besets my waking hours, are accomplices in all this, comical and ineffectual though you pretend to be. As for that creature" (here she gestured toward the sleeping Alice), "she knows only too well the implications of her presence here with that changeling, and how these constitute a reflection on my inward character as illustrated in my outward appearance, such as this spangled gown and these tangled tresses, meant to epitomize the confusion which is the one source of my living being, but which in these ambiguous surroundings, neither true fantasy nor clean-cut reality, keeps me at bay until I can no longer see the woman I once was. I shall not rest until I have erased all of this from my thoughts, or (which is more likely) incorporated it into the confusing scheme I have erected around me for my support and glorification."

At this there was some whispering and apprehensive regrouping among the hobos; meanwhile Alice and the pig slept on oblivious, the latter's snores having become more relaxed and peaceful than before. Mania continued to stride back and forth, impetuously stabbing her wand into the ground. Suddenly a black horse with a rider swathed in a dark cloak and with a dark sombrero pulled down over his face approached quickly along a path leading through the trees from the right of the stage. Without dismounting or revealing his face the stranger accosted the lady:

STRANGER: Why do you pace back and forth like this, ignoring the critical reality of this scene, or pretending that it is a monstrosity of reason sent by some envious commonsensical deity to confound and humiliate you? You might have been considered beautiful, and an ornament even to such a curious setting as this, had you not persisted in spoiling the clear and surprising outline of your character, and leading around this hideous misshapen beast as though to scare off any who might have approached you so as to admire you.

MANIA: I am as I am, and in that I am happy, and care nothing for the opinion of others. The very idea of the idea others might entertain of me is as a poison to me, pushing me to flee farther into wastes even less hospitable and more treacherously combined of irregular elements than this one. As for my pet hyena, beauty is in the eye of the beholder; at least, I find him beautiful, and, unlike other beasts, he has the ability to laugh and sneer at the spectacle around us.

STRANGER: Come with me, and I will take you into the presence of one at whose court beauty and irrationality reign alternately, and never tread on each other's toes as do your unsightly followers [more whispering and gesturing among the hobos], where your own pronounced contours may flourish and be judged for what they are worth, while the anomalies of the room you happen to be in or the disturbing letters and phone calls that hamper your free unorthodox development will melt away like crystal rivulets leaving a glacier, and you may dwell in the accident of your character forever.

MANIA: You speak well, and if all there is as you say, I am convinced and will accompany you gladly. But before doing so I must ask you two questions. First, what is the name of her to whose palace you purpose to lead me; and second, may I bring my hyena along?

STRANGER: As to the first question, that I may not answer now, but you'll find out soon enough. As to the second, the answer is yes, providing it behaves itself.

The lady mounted the stranger's steed with his help, and sat sideways, with the hyena on its chain trotting along behind them. As they rode back into the woods the forest faded away and the scene became an immense metallic sky in which a huge lead-colored sphere or disc—impossible to determine which—seemed to float midway between the proscenium and the floor of stage. At right and left behind the footlights some of the hobos, reduced almost to midget size, rushed back and forth gesticulating at the strange orb that hung above them; with them mingled a few nursery-rhyme characters such as the Knave of Hearts and the Pie Man, who seemed to be looking around uneasily for Simon. All were puzzled or terrified by the strange new apparition, which seemed to grow darker and denser while the sky surrounding it stayed the same white-metal color.

Alice, awakening from her slumber, stood up and joined the group at the front of the stage, leaving the pig in its baby clothes to scamper off into the wings. Wiping away some strands of hair that had fallen across her forehead and seeming to become aware of the changed landscape around her, she turned to the others and asked, "What happens now?"

In reply, Jack Horner, who had been gazing at the camera in his hand with an expression of ironic detachment, like Hamlet contemplating the skull of Yorick, jerked his head upward toward the banner, whose scarlet motto still blazed brightly though the trees that supported it were fast fading in the glare from the sky. Alice too looked up, noticing it for the first time.

"I see," she said at length. "A process of duration has been set in motion around us, though there is no indication I can see that any of us is involved in it. If that is the case, what conclusion are we to draw? Why are we here, if even such a nebulous concept as 'here' is to be allowed us? What are we to do?"

At this the Knave of Hearts stepped forward and cast his eyes modestly toward the ground. "I see separate, soft pain, lady," he said. "The likes of these"—he indicated with a sweep of his arm the group of hobos and others who had subsided into worried reclining poses in the background—"who know not what they are, or what they mean, I isolate from the serious business of creatures such as we, both more ordinary and more distinguished than the common herd of anesthetized earthlings. It is so that we may question more acutely the sphere into which we have been thrust, that threatens to smother us at every second and above which we rise triumphant with each breath we draw. At least, that is the way I see it."

"Then you are a fool as well as a knave," Jack answered angrily, "since you don't seem to realize that the sphere is escaping us, rather than the reverse, and that in a moment it will have become one less thing to carry."

As he spoke the stage grew very dark, so that the circle in the sky finally seemed light by contrast, while a soft wail arose from the instruments in the orchestra pit.

"I suspect the mischief of Mercury in all this," muttered Jack, keeping a weather eye on the heavens. "For though some believe Hermes' lineage to be celestial, others maintain that he is of infernal origin, and emerges on earth to do the errands of Pluto and Proserpine on the rare occasions when they have business here."

The lights slowly came up again, revealing a perspective view of a busy main street in a large American city. The dark outline of the disc still persisted in the sky, yet the climate seemed warm and sunny, though there were Christmas decorations strung across the street and along the facades of department stores, and on a nearby street corner stood a Salvation Army Santa Claus with his bell and cauldron. It could have been downtown Los Angeles in the late 30s or early- to mid-40s, judging from the women's fashions and the models of cars that crawled along the street as though pulled by invisible strings.

Walking in place on a sidewalk which was actually a treadmill moving toward the back of the stage was a couple in their early thirties. Mania (for the woman was none other than she) was dressed in the style of Joan Crawford in *Mildred Pierce,* in a severe suit with padded shoulders and a pillbox with a veil crowning the pincurls of her upswept hairdo, which also cascaded to her shoulders, ending in more pincurls. Instead of the sheaf of gladioli she now clutched a black handbag suspended on a strap over her shoulder, and in place of the hyena, one of those *little white dogs* on the end of a leash kept sniffing the legs of pedestrians who were in truth mere celluloid phantoms, part of the process shot which made up the whole downtown backdrop. The man at her side wore a broad-brimmed hat, loose-fitting sport coat and baggy gabardine slacks; he bore a certain resemblance to the actor Bruce Bennett but closer inspection revealed him to be the statue of Mercury, with the paint still peeling from his face around the empty eye sockets. At first it looked as though the two were enjoying the holiday atmosphere and drinking in the sights and sounds of the city. Gradually, however, Mania's expression darkened; finally she stopped in the middle of the sidewalk and pulled at her escort's sleeve.

"Listen, Herman," she said, perhaps addressing Bruce Bennett by his real name, Herman Brix, "you said you were going to take me to this swell place and all, where I was supposed to meet a lot of interesting people who could help me in my career. All we do is walk down this dopey street looking in store windows and waiting for the stoplights to change. Is this your idea of a good time?"

"But this is all part of it, hon, part of what I promised you," Mercury rejoined. "Don't you feel the atmosphere yet? That powder-blue sky of the eternal postcard, with the haze of mountain peaks barely visible; the salmon-colored pavement with its little green and blue cars that look so still though they are supposed to be in motion? The window shoppers, people like you and me . . . ?"

"*That's* what I thought," Mania pouted, stamping one of her feet in its platform shoe so loudly that several of the extras turned to look. "Atmosphere—that's what it was all along, wasn't it? A question of ambience, poetry, something like that. I might as well have stayed in my cave for all the good it's going to do me. After all, I'm used to not blending in with the environment—it's my business not to. But I thought you were going to take me away from all that, to some place where scenery made no difference any more, where I could be what everybody accuses me of being and what I suppose I must be—my tired, tyrannical self, as separate from local color as geometry is from the hideous verticals of these avenues and buildings and the festoons that extend them into the shrinking consciousness. Have you forgotten the words of St. Augustine: 'Multiply in your imagination the light of the sun, make it greater and brighter as you will, a thousand times or out of number. God will not be there'?"

Then we all realized what should have been obvious from the start: that the setting would go on evolving eternally, rolling its waves across our vision like an ocean, each one new yet recognizably a part of the same series, which was creation itself. Scenes from movies, plays, operas, television; decisive or little-known episodes from history; prenatal and other early memories from our own solitary, separate pasts; events yet to come from life or art; calamities or moments of relaxation; universal or personal tragedies; or little vignettes from daily life that you just had to stop and laugh at, they were so funny, like the dog chasing its tail on the living-room rug. The sunny city in California faded away and another scene took its place, and another and another. And the corollary of all this was that we would go on witnessing these tableaux, not that anything prevented us from leaving the theater, but there was no alternative to our interest in finding out what would happen next. This was the only thing that mattered for us, so we stayed on although we could have stood up and walked away in disgust at any given moment. And event followed event according to an inner logic of its own. We saw the set for the first act of *La Bohème,* picturesque poverty on a scale large enough to fill the stages of the world's greatest opera houses, from Leningrad to Buenos Aires, punctuated only by a skylight, an easel or two and a stove with a smoking stovepipe, but entirely filled up with the boisterous and sincere camaraderie of Rodolfo, Marcello, Colline and their friends; a ripe, generous atmosphere into which Mimi is introduced like the first splinter of unavoidable death, and the scene melts imperceptibly into the terrace of the Café Momus, where the friends have gathered to drink and discuss philosophy, when suddenly the blond actress who had earlier been seen as Daffy Down Dilly returns as Musetta, mocking her elderly protector and pouring out peal after peal of deathless melody concerning the joys and advantages of life as a *grisette,* meanwhile clutching a small velvet handbag in which the contour of a small revolver was clearly visible, for as we well knew from previous experience, she was the symbol of the unexpectedness and exuberance of death, which we had waited to have come round again and which we would be meeting many times more during the course of the performance. There were murky scenes from television with a preponderance of excerpts from Jacques Cousteau documentaries with snorkeling figures disappearing down aqueous perspectives, past arrangements of coral still-lifes and white, fanlike creatures made of snowy tripe whose trailing vinelike tentacles could paralyze a man for life, and a seeming excess of silver bubbles constantly being emitted from here and there to sweep upward to the top of the screen, where they vanished. There were old clips from *Lucy, Lassie* and *The Waltons;* there was Walter Cronkite bidding us an urgent good evening years ago. Mostly there were just moments: a street corner viewed from above, bare branches flailing the sky, a child in a doorway, a painted Pennsylvania Dutch chest, a full moon disappearing behind a dark cloud to the accompaniment of a Japanese flute, a ballerina in a frosted white dress lifted up into the light.

Always behind it the circle in the sky remained fixed like a ghost on a television screen. The setting was now the last act of Ibsen's *When We*

Dead Awaken: "A wild, broken mountaintop, with a sheer precipice behind. To the right tower snowy peaks, losing themselves high up in drifting mist. To the left, on a scree, stands an old, tumbledown hut. It is early morning. Dawn is breaking, the sun has not yet risen." Here the disc in the sky could begin to take on the properties of the sun that had been denied it for so long: as though made of wet wool, it began little by little to soak up and distribute light. The figure of Mercury had become both more theatrical and more human: no longer a statue, he was draped in a freshly laundered chlamys that set off his well-formed but slight physique; the broad-brimmed *petasus* sat charmingly on his curls. He sat, legs spread apart, on an iron park bench, digging absent-mindedly at the ground with his staff from which leaves rather then serpents sprouted, occasionally bending over to scratch the part of his heel behind the strap of his winged sandal. The morning mists were evaporating; the light was becoming the ordinary yellow daylight of the theater. Resting both hands on his staff, he leaned forward to address the audience, cocking his head in the shrewd bumpkin manner of a Will Rogers.

"So you think I have it, after all, or that I've found it? And you may be right. But I still say that what counts isn't the particular set of circumstances, but how we adapt ourselves to them, and you all must know that by now, watching all these changes of scene and scenery till you feel it's coming out of your ears. *I* know how it is; I've been everywhere, bearing messages to this one and that one, often steaming them open to see what's inside and getting a good dose of *that* too, in addition to the peaks of Tartarus which I might be flying over at the time. It's like sleeping too close to the edge of the bed—sometimes you're in danger of falling out on one side and sometimes on the other, but rarely do you fall out, and in general your dreams proceed pretty much in the normal way dreams have of proceeding. I still think the old plain way is better: the ideas, speeches, arguments—whatever you want to call 'em— on one hand, and strongly written scenes and fully fleshed-out characters in flannel suits and leg-o'-mutton sleeves on the other. For the new moon is most beautiful viewed through burnt twigs and the last few decrepit leaves still clinging to them."

Suddenly he glanced upward toward the scree and noticed a girl in a Victorian shirtwaist and a straw boater hat moving timidly down the path through the now wildly swirling mists. She was giggling silently with embarrassment and wonder, meanwhile clasping an old-fashioned kodak, which she had pointed at Mercury.

"It is Sabrina," he said. "The wheel has at last come full circle, and it is the simplicity of an encounter that was meant all along. It happened ever so many years ago, when we were children, and could have happened so many times since! But it isn't our fault that it has chosen this moment and this moment only, to repeat itself! For even if it does menace us directly, *it's exciting all the same!*"

And the avalanche fell and fell, and continues to fall even today.

· THE PATH TO
THE WHITE MOON ·

There were little farmhouses there they
Looked like farmhouses yes without very much land
And trees, too many trees and a mistake
Built into each thing rather charmingly
But once you have seen a thing you have to move on

You have to lie in the grass
And play with your hair, scratch yourself
And then the space of this behavior, the air,
Has suddenly doubled
And you have grown to fill the extra place
Looking back at the small, fallen shelter that was

If a stream winds through all this
Alongside an abandoned knitting mill it will not
Say where it has been
The time unfolds like music trapped on the page
Unable to tell the story again
Raging

Where the winters grew white we went outside
To look at things again, putting on more clothes
This too an attempt to define
How we were being in all the surroundings
Big ones sleepy ones
Underwear and hats speak to us
As though we were cats
Dependent and independent
There were shouted instructions
Grayed in the morning

Keep track of us
It gets to be so exciting but so big too

And we have ways to define but not the terms
Yet
We know what is coming, that we are moving
Dangerously and gracefully
Toward the resolution of time
Blurred but alive with many separate meanings
Inside this conversation

· DITTO, KIDDO ·

How brave you are! *Sometimes.* And the injunction
Still stands, a plain white wall. More unfinished business.
But isn't that just the nature of business, someone else said, breezily.
You can't just pick up in the middle of it, and then leave off.
What if you do listen to it over and over, until

It becomes part of your soul, foreign matter that belongs there?
I ask you so many times to think about this rupture you are
Proceeding with, this revolution. And still time
Is draped around your shoulders. The weather report
Didn't mention rain, and you are ass-deep in it, so?
Find other predictions. These are good for throwing away,
Yesterday's newspapers, and those of the weeks before that spreading
Backward, away, almost in perfect order. It's all there
To interrupt your speaking. There is no other use to the past

Until those times when, driving abruptly off a road
Into a field you sit still and conjure the hours.
It was for this we made the small talk, the lies,
And whispered them over to give each the smell of truth,
But now, like biting devalued currency, they become possessions
As the stars come out. And the ridiculous machine
Still trickles mottoes: "Plastered again . . . " "from our house
To your house . . . " We wore these for a while, and they became us.

Each day seems full of itself, and yet it is only
A few colored beans and some straw lying on a dirt floor
In a mote-filled shaft of light. There *was* room. Yes,
And you have created it by going away. Somewhere, someone
Listens for your laugh, swallows it like a drink of cool water,
Neither happy nor aghast. And the stance, that post standing there, is you.

· INTRODUCTION ·

To be a writer and write things
You must have experiences you can write about.
Just living won't do. I have a theory
About masterpieces, how to make them
At very little expense, and they're every
Bit as good as the others. You can
Use the same materials of the dream, at last.

It's a kind of game with no losers and only one
Winner—you. First, pain gets
Flashed back through the story and the story
Comes out backwards and woof-side up. This is
No one's story! At least they think that
For a time and the story is architecture
Now, and then history of a diversified kind.
A vacant episode during which the bricks got
Repointed and browner. And it ends up
Nobody's, there is nothing for any of us
Except that fretful vacillating around the central
Question that brings us closer,
For better and worse, for all this time.

· I SEE, SAID THE BLIND MAN,
AS HE PUT DOWN HIS HAMMER AND SAW ·

There is some charm in that old music
He'd fall for when the night wind released it—
Pleasant to be away; the stones fall back;
The hill of gloom in place over the roar
Of the kitchens but with remembrance like a bright patch
Of red in a bunch of laundry. But will the car
Ever pull away and spunky at all times he'd
Got the mission between the ladder
And the slices of bread someone had squirted astrology over
Until it took the form of a man, obtuse, out of pocket
Perhaps, probably standing there.

Can't you see how we need these far-from-restful pauses?
And in the wind neighbors and such agree
It's a hard thing, a milestone of sorts in some way?
So that the curtains contribute what charm they can
To the spectacle: an overflowing cesspool
Among the memoirs of court life, the candy, cigarettes,
And what else. What kind is it, is there more than one
Kind, are people forever going to be at the edge
Of things, even the nice ones, and when it happens
Will we all be alone together? The armor
Of these thoughts laughs at itself
Yet the distances are always growing
With everything between, in between.

Another blueprint: some foxing, woolly the foliage
On this dusky shrine
Under the glass dome on the spinet
To make it seem all these voices were once one.
Outside, the rout continues:
The clash erupting to the very door, but the
Door is secure. There is room here still
For thoughts like ferns being integrated
Into another system, something to scare the night away,
And when morning comes they have gone, only the dew
Remains. What more did we want anyway?
I'm sorry. We believe there is something more than attributes
And coefficients, that the giant erection
Is something more than the peg on which our lives hang,
Ours, yours . . . The core is not concern
But for afternoon busy with blinds open, restless with
Search-and-destroy missions, the approach to business is new
And ancient and mellow at the same time. For them to gain
Their end, the peace of fireworks on a vanishing sky,
We have to bother. Please welcome the three insane interviewers
Each with his astrolabe and question.
And the days drain into the sea.

· 37 HAIKU ·

Old-fashioned shadows hanging down, that difficulty in love too soon

Some star or other went out, and you, thank you for your book and year

Something happened in the garage and I owe it for the blood traffic

Too low for nettles but it is exactly the way people think and feel

And I think there's going to be even more but waist-high

Night occurs dimmer each time with the pieces of light smaller and squarer

You have original artworks hanging on the walls oh I said edit

You nearly undermined the brush I now place against the ball field arguing

That love was a round place and will still be there two years from now

And it is a dream sailing in a dark unprotected cove

Pirates imitate the ways of ordinary people myself for instance

Planted over and over that land has a bitter aftertaste

A blue anchor grains of grit in a tall sky sewing

He is a monster like everyone else but what do you do if you're a monster

Like him feeling him come from far away and then go down to his car

The wedding was enchanted everyone was glad to be in it

What trees, tools, why ponder socks on the premises

Come to the edge of the barn the property really begins there

In a smaller tower shuttered and put away there

You lay aside your hair like a book that is too important to read now

Why did witches pursue the beast from the eight sides of the country

A pencil on glass—shattered! The water runs down the drain

In winter sometimes you see those things and also in summer

A child must go down it must stand and last

Too late the last express passes through the dust of gardens

A vest—there is so much to tell about even in the side rooms

Hesitantly, it built up and passed quickly without unlocking

There are some places kept from the others and are separate, they never exist

I lost my ridiculous accent without acquiring another

In Buffalo, Buffalo she was praying, the nights stick together like pages in an
old book

The dreams descend like cranes on gilded, forgetful wings

What is the past, what is it all for? A mental sandwich?

Did you say, hearing the schooner overhead, we turned back to the weir?

In rags and crystals, sometimes with a shred of sense, an odd dignity

The boy must have known the particles fell through the house after him

All in all we were taking our time, the sea returned—no more pirates

I inch and only sometimes as far as the twisted pole gone in spare colors

· HAIBUN ·

Wanting to write something I could think only of my own ideas, though you surely have your separate, private being in some place I will never walk through. And then of the dismal space between us, filled though it may be with interesting objects, standing around like trees waiting to be discovered. It may be that this is the intellectual world. But if so, what poverty—even the discoveries yet to be made, and which shall surprise us, even us. It must be heightened somehow, but not to brutality. That is an invention and not a true instinct, and this must never be invented. Yet I am forced to invent, even if during the process I become a *songe-creux,* inaccurate dreamer, and these inventions are then to be claimed by the first person who happens on them. I'm hoping that homosexuals not yet born get to inquire about it, inspect the whole random collection as though it were a sphere. Isn't the point of pain the possibility it brings of being able to get along without pain, for awhile, of manipulating our marionette-like limbs in the straitjacket of air, and so to have written something? Unprofitable shifts of light and dark in the winter sky address this dilemma very directly. In time to come we shall perceive them as the rumpled linen or scenery through which we did walk once, for a short time, during some sort of vacation. It is a frostbitten, brittle world but once you are inside it you want to stay there always.

The year—not yet abandoned but a living husk, a lesson

. . . and can see the many hidden ways merit drains out of the established and internationally acclaimed containers, like a dry patch of sky. It is an affair of some enormity. The sky is swathed in a rich, gloomy and finally silly grandeur, like drapery in a portrait by Lebrun. This is to indicate that our actions in this tiny, tragic platform are going to be more than usually infinitesimal, given the superhuman scale on which we have to operate, and also that we should not take any comfort from the inanity of our situation; we are still valid creatures with a job to perform, and the arena facing us, though titanic, hasn't rolled itself beyond the notion of dimension. It isn't suitable, and it's here. Shadows are thrown out at the base of things at right angles to the regular shadows that are already there, pointing in the correct direction. They are faint but not invisible, and it seems appropriate to start intoning the litany of dimensions there, at the base of a sapling spreading its lines in two directions. The temperature hardens, and things like the smell and the mood of water are suddenly more acute, and may help us. We will never know whether they did.

Water, a bossa nova, a cello is centred, the light behind the library

I was swimming with the water at my back, funny thing is it was real this time. I mean this time it was working. We weren't too far from shore, the guides hadn't noticed yet. Always you work out of the possibility of being injured, but this time, all the new construction, the new humiliation, you have to see it. Guess it's OK to take a look. But a cup of tea—you wouldn't want to spill it. And a grapefruit (spelled "grapfruit" on the small, painstakingly lettered card) after a while, and the new gray suit. Then more, and more, it was a kind of foliage or some built-in device to trip you. Make you fall. The encounter with the silence of permissiveness stretching away like a moonlit sea to the horizon, whatever that really is. *They* want you to like it. And you honor them in liking it. You cause pleasure before sleep insists, draws over to where you may yet be. And some believe this is merely a detail. And they may be right. And we may be the whole of which all that truly happens is only peelings and shreds of bark. Not that we are too much more than these. Remember they don't have to thank you for it either.

The subtracted sun, all I'm going by here, with the boy, this new
    maneuver is less than the letter in the wind

Dark at four again. Sadly I negotiate the almost identical streets as little by little they are obliterated under a rain of drips and squiggles of light. Their message of universal brotherhood through suffering is taken from the top, the pedal held down so that the first note echoes throughout the piece without becoming exactly audible. It collects over different parts of the city and the drift in those designated parts is different from elsewhere. It is a man, it was one all along. No it isn't. It is a man with the conscience of a woman, always coming out of something, turning to look at you, wondering about a possible reward. How sweet to my sorrow is this man's knowledge in his way of coming, the brotherhood that will surely result under now darkened skies.

The pressing, pressing urgent whispers, pushing on, seeing directly

Bring them all back to life, with white gloves on, out of the dream in which they are still alive. Loosen the adhesive bonds that tie them to the stereotypes of the dead, clichés like the sound of running water. Abruptly it was winter again. A slope several football fields wide sprang out of the invisible foreground, the one behind me, and unlaced its barren provocation upwards, with flair and menace, at a 20-degree angle—the ascending night and also the voice in it that means to be heard, a pagoda of which is visible at the left horizon, not meaning much: the flurry of a cold wind. We're in it too chortled the rowanberries. And how fast so much aggressiveness unfolded, like a swiftly flowing, silent stream. Along its banks world history presented itself as a series of translucent tableaux, fading imperceptibly into one another, so that the taking of Quebec by the British in 1629 melts into the lollipop tints of Marquette and Joliet crossing the mouth of the Missouri River. But at the center a rope of distress twists itself ever tighter around some of the possessions we brought from the old place and were going to arrange here. And what about the courteous but dispassionate gaze of an armed messenger on his way from someplace to someplace else that is the speech of all the old, resurrected loves, tinged with respect, caring to see that you are no longer alone now in this dream you chose. The dark yellowish flow of light drains out of the slanted dish of the sky and from the masses of the loved a tremendous chant arises: We are viable! And so back into the city with its glimmers of possibility like Broadway nights of notoriety and the warm syrup of embarrassed and insistent proclamations of all kinds of tidings that made you what you were in the world and made the world for you, only diminished once it had been seen and become the object of further speculation leading like railroad ties out of the present inconclusive sphere into the world of two dimensions.

A terminus, pole fringed with seaweed at its base, a cracked memory

To be involved in every phase of directing, acting, producing and so on must be infinitely rewarding. Just as when a large, fat, lazy frog hops off his lily pad like a spitball propelled by a rubber band and disappears into the water of the pond with an enthusiastic plop. It cannot be either changed or improved on. So too with many of life's little less-than-pleasurable experiences, like the rain that falls and falls for so long that no one can remember when it began or what weather used to be, or cares much either; they are much too busy trying to plug holes in ceilings or emptying pails and other containers and then quickly pushing them back to catch the overflow. But nobody seems eager to accord ideal status to this situation and I, for one, would love to know why. Don't we realize that after all these centuries that are now starting to come apart like moldy encyclopedias in some abandoned, dusty archive that we have to take the bitter with the sweet or soon all distinctions will be submerged by the tide of tepid approval of everything that is beginning to gather force and direction as well? And when its mighty roar threatens in earnest the partially submerged bridges and cottages, picks up the floundering cattle to deposit them in trees and so on to who knows what truly horrible mischief, it will be time, then, to genuinely rethink this and come up with true standards of evaluation, only it will be too late of course, too late for anything but the satisfaction that lasts only just so long. A pity, though. Meanwhile I lift my glass to these black-and-silver striped nights. I believe that the rain never drowned sweeter, more prosaic things than those we have here, now, and I believe this is going to have to be enough.

Striped hair, inquisitive gloves, a face, some woman named Ernestine
    Throckmorton, white opera glasses and more

· VARIATION ON A NOEL ·

> "... when the snow lay round about,
> deep and crisp and even ..."

A year away from the pigpen, and look at him.
A thirsty unit by an upending stream,
Man doctors, God supplies the necessary medication
If elixir were to be found in the world's dolor, where is none.

A thirsty unit by an upending stream,
Ashamed of the moon of everything that hides too little of her nakedness—
If elixir were to be found in the world's dolor, where is none,
Our emancipation should be great and steady.

Ashamed of the moon, of everything that hides too little of her nakedness—
The twilight prayers begin to emerge on a country crossroads.
Our emancipation should be great and steady
As crossword puzzles done in this room, this after-effect.

The twilight prayers begin to emerge on a country crossroads
Where no sea contends with the interest of the cherry trees.
As crossword puzzles done in this room, this after-effect,
I see the whole thing written down.

Where no sea contends with the interest of the cherry trees
Everything but love was abolished. It stayed on, a stepchild.
I see the whole thing written down:
Business, a lack of drama. Whatever the partygoing public needs.

Everything but love was abolished. It stayed on, a stepchild.
The bent towers of the playroom advanced to something like openness,
Business, a lack of drama. Whatever the partygoing public needs
To be kind, and to forget, passing through the next doors.

The bent towers of the playroom advanced to something like openness.
But if you heard it, and you didn't want it
To be kind, and to forget, passing through the next doors
(For we believe him not exiled from the skies) ...

But if you heard it, and if you didn't want it,
Why do I call to you after all this time?
For we believe him not exiled from the skies.
Because I wish to give only what the specialist can give,

Why do I call to you after all this time?
Your own friends, running for mayor, behaving outlandishly
Because I wish to give only what the specialist can give,
Spend what they care to.

Your own friends, running for mayor, behaving outlandishly,
(And I have known him cheaply)
Spend what they care to.
A form of ignorance, you might say. Let's leave that though.

And I have known him cheaply.
Agree to remove all that concern, another exodus—
A form of ignorance, you might say. Let's leave that though.
The mere whiteness was a blessing, taking us far.

Agree to remove all that concern, another exodus.
A year away from the pigpen, and look at him.
The mere whiteness was a blessing, taking us far.
Man doctors, God supplies the necessary medication.

· STAFFAGE ·

Sir, I am one of a new breed
Of inquisitive pest in love with the idea
Of our integrity, programming us over dark seas
Into small offices, where we sit and compete
With you, on your own time.
We want only to be recognized for what we are;
Everything else is secondary.
Consequently, I shall sit on your doorstep
Till you notice me. I'm still too young
To be overlooked, yet not old enough to qualify
For full attention. I'll flesh out
The thin warp of your dreams, make them meatier,
Nuttier. And when a thin pall gathers
Leading finally to outraged investigation
Into what matters next, I'll be there
On the other side.
                    Half of me I give
To do with as you wish—scold, ignore, forget for awhile.
The other half I keep, and shall feel
Fully rewarded if you pass by this offer
Without recognizing it, receding deliberately
Into the near distance, which speaks no longer
Of loss, but of brevity rather: short naps, keeping fit.

The first movie I ever saw was the Walt Disney cartoon *The Three Little Pigs*. My grandmother took me to it. It was back in the days when you went "downtown." There was a second feature, with live actors, called *Bring 'Em Back Alive*, a documentary about the explorer Frank Buck. In this film you saw a python swallow a live pig. This wasn't scary. In fact, it seemed quite normal, the sort of thing you *would* see in a movie—"reality."

A little later we went downtown again to see a movie of *Alice in Wonderland*, also with live actors. This wasn't very surprising either. I think I knew something about the story; maybe it had been read to me. That wasn't why it wasn't surprising, though. The reason was that these famous movie actors, like W. C. Fields and Gary Cooper, were playing different roles, and even though I didn't know who they were, they were obviously important for doing other kinds of acting, and so it didn't seem strange that they should be acting in a special way like this, pretending to be characters that people already knew about from a book. In other words, I imagined specialties for them just from having seen this one example. And I was right, too, though not about the film, which I liked. Years later I saw it when I was grown up and thought it was awful. How could I have been wrong the first time? I knew it wasn't inexperience, because somehow I was experienced the first time I saw a movie. It was as though my taste had changed, though I had not, and I still can't help feeling that I was right the first time, when I was still relatively unencumbered by my experience.

I forget what were the next movies I saw and will skip ahead to one I saw when I was grown up, *The Lonedale Operator*, a silent short by D. W. Griffith, made in 1911 and starring Blanche Sweet. Although I was in my twenties when I saw it at the Museum of Modern Art, it seems as remote from me in time as my first viewing of *Alice in Wonderland*. I can remember almost none of it, and the little I can remember may have been in another Griffith short, *The Lonely Villa*, which may have been on the same program. It seems that Blanche Sweet was a heroic telephone operator who managed to get through to the police and foil some gangsters who were trying to rob a railroad depot, though I also see this living room—small, though it was supposed to be in a large house—with Mary Pickford running around, and this may have been a scene in *The Lonely Villa*. At that moment the memories stop, and terror, or tedium, sets in. It's hard to tell which is which in this memory, because the boredom of living in a lonely place or having a lonely job, and even of being so far in the past and having to wear those funny uncomfortable clothes and hairstyles is terrifying, more so than the intentional scariness of the plot, the criminals, whoever they were.

Imagine that innocence (Lilian Harvey) encounters romance (Willy Fritsch) in the home of experience (Albert Basserman). From there it is only a step to terror, under the dripping boughs outside. Anything can change as fast as it wants to, and in doing so may pass through a more or less terrible phase, but the true terror is in the swiftness of changing, forward or backward, slipping always just beyond our control. The actors are like people on drugs, though they aren't doing anything unusual—as a matter of fact, they are performing brilliantly.

I am beginning to wonder
Whether this alternative to
Sitting back and doing something quiet
Is the clever initiative it seemed. It's
Also relaxation and sunlight branching into
Passionate melancholy, jealousy of something unknown;
And our minds, parked in the sky over New York,
Are nonetheless responsible. Nights
When the paper comes
And you walk around the block
Wrenching yourself from the lover every five minutes
And it hurts, yet nothing is ever really clean
Or two-faced. You are losing your grip
And there are still flowers and compliments in the air:
"How did you like the last one?"
"Was I good?" "I think it stinks."

It's a question of questions, first:
The nuts-and-bolts kind you know you can answer
And the impersonal ones you answer almost without meaning to:
"My greatest regret." "What keeps the world from falling down."
And then the results are brilliant:
Someone is summoned to a name, and soon
A roomful of people becomes dense and contoured
And words come out of the wall
To batter the rhythm of generation following on generation.

And I see once more how everything
Must be up to me: here a calamity to be smoothed away
Like ringlets, there the luck of uncoding
This singular cipher of primary
And secondary colors, and the animals
With us in the ark, happy to be there as it settles
Into an always more violent sea.

· CUPS WITH BROKEN HANDLES ·

So much variation
In what is basically a one-horse town:
Part of me frivolous, part intentionally crude,
And part unintentionally thoughtless.
Modesty and false modesty stroll hand in hand
Like twin girls. But there are more abstract things too
That play a larger role. The intense, staccato repetitions
Of whatever. You don't know and we don't know either.

From there it's a big, though necessary, leap to
The more subtly conceptual conditionings: your opinion
Of you shaped in the vacuum-form of suppositions,
Correct or false, of others, and how we can never be ourselves
While so much of us is going on in the minds of other people,
People you meet on the street who greet you strangely
As though remembering a recent trip to the Bahamas
And say things like: "It is broken. But we'd heard
You heard too. Isn't it too bad about old things, old schools,
Old dishes, with nothing to do but sit and wait
Their turn. Meanwhile you're
Looking stretched again, concentrated, as you do not pass
From point A to point B but merely speculate
On how it would be, and in that instant
Do appear to be traveling, though we all
Stay home, don't we. Our strength lies
In the potential for motion, not in accomplishments, and it gets
Used up too, which is, in a way, more effective."

· JUST SOMEONE
YOU SAY HI TO ·

But what about me, I
Wondered as the parachute released
Its carrousel into the sky over me?
I never think about it
Unless I think about it all the time
And therefore don't know except in dreams
How I behave, what I mean to myself.
Should I wonder more
How I'm doing, inquire more after you
With the face like a birthday present
I am unwrapping as the parachute wanders
Through us, across blue ridges brown with autumn leaves?

People are funny—they see it
And then it's that that they want.
No wonder we look out from ourselves
To the other person going on.
What about my end of the stick?
I keep thinking if I could get through you
I'd get back to me at a further stage
Of this journey, but the tent flaps fall,
The parachute won't land, only drift sideways.
The carnival never ends; the apples,
The land, are duly tucked away
And we are left with only sensations of ourselves
And the dry otherness, like a clenched fist
Around the throttle as we go down, sideways and down.

· THEY LIKE ·

They like to drink beer and wave their hands and whistle
Much as human beings everywhere do. Dark objects loom
Out of the night, attracted by the light of conversations,
And they take note of that, thinking how funny everything is.

It was a long time ago that you began. The dawn was brittle
And open, and things stayed in it for a long time as images
After the projecting urge had left. In the third year a tension
Arose like smoke on the horizon, but it was quickly subdued.
And now in the fifth year you return with tears
That are, I understand, a formality, to seal the naked time
And pave it over so that it may be walked across. The day with
Its straw flowers and dried fruits is for "putting up" too.

At a corner you meet the one who makes you glad, like a stranger
Off on some business. Come again soon. I will,
I will. Only this time let your serious proposals stick out
Into the bay a considerable distance, like piers. Remember
I am not the stranger I seem to be, only casual
And ruthless, but kind. Kind and strange. It isn't a warning.

The flares in the lower sky are no longer ambitious
But a steady, droning red. That's my middle initial up there,
Hanging over a populous city. Flowers and fires everywhere,
A warning surely. But they all lead their lives appropriately
Into desperation, and nobody seems surprised. Only the story
Stays behind, when they go away, sitting on a stone. It grew and grew.

Sometimes I get radiant drunk when I think of and/or look at you,
Upstaged by our life, with me in it.
And other mornings too
Your care is like a city, with the uncomfortable parts
Evasive, and difficult to connect with the plan
That was, and the green diagonals of the rain kind of
Fudging to rapidly involve everything that stood out,
And doing so in an illegal way, but it doesn't matter,
It's rapture that counts, and what little
There is of it is seldom aboveboard,
That's its nature,
What we take our cue from.
It masquerades as worry, first, then as self-possession
In which I am numb, imagining I am this vision
Of ships stuck on the tarpaper of an urban main,
At night, coal stars glinting,
And you the ruby lights hung far above on pylons,
Seeming to own the night and the nearer reaches
Of a civilization we feel as ours,
The lining of our old doing.

I can walk away from you
Because I know I can always call, and in the end we will
Be irresolutely joined,
Laughing over this alphabet of connivance
That never goes on too long, because outside
My city there is wind, and burning straw and other things that don't coincide,
To which we'll be condemned, perhaps, some day.
Now our peace is in our assurance
And has that savor,
Its own blind deduction
Of whatever would become of us if
We were alone, to nurture on this shore some fable
To block out that other whose remote being

Becomes every day a little more sentient and more suavely realized.
I'll believe it when the police pay *you* off.
In the meantime there are so many things not to believe in
We can make a hobby of them, as long as we continue to uphold
The principle of private property.
So what if ours is planted with tin-can trees
It's better than a forest full of parked cars with the lights out,
Because the effort of staying back to side with someone
For whom number is everything
Will finally unplug the dark
And the black acacias stand out as symbols, lovers
Of what men will at last stop doing to each other
When we can be quiet, and start counting sheep to stay awake together.

Many colors will take you to themselves
But now I want someone to tell me how to get home.
The way back there is streaked and stippled,
A shaded place. It belongs where it is going

Not where it is. The flowers don't talk to Ida now.
They speak only the language of flowers,
Saying things like, How hard I tried to get there.
It must mean I'm not here yet. But you,
You seem so formal, so serious. You can't read poetry,
Not the way they taught us back in school.

Returning to the point was always the main thing, then.
Did we ever leave it? I don't think so. It was our North Pole.
We skulked and hungered there for years, and now,
Like dazzled insects skimming the bright airs,
You are back on the road again, the path leading
Vigorously upward, through intelligent and clear spaces.
They don't make rocks like us any more.

And holding on to the thread, fine as a cobweb, but incredibly strong,
Each of us advances into his own labyrinth.
The gift of invisibility
Has been granted to all but the gods, so we say such things,
Filling the road up with colors, faces,
Tender speeches, until they feed us to the truth.

· DARLENE'S HOSPITAL ·

The hospital: it wasn't her idea
That the colors should slide muddy from the brush
And spew their random evocations everywhere,
Provided that things should pick up next season.
It was a way of living, to her way of thinking.
She took a job, it wasn't odd.
But then, backing through the way many minds had been made up,
It came again, the color, always a color
Climbing the apple of the sky, often
A secret lavender place you weren't supposed to look into.
And then a sneeze would come along
Or soon we'd be too far out from shore, on a milky afternoon
Somewhere in late August with the paint flaking off,
The lines of traffic flowing like mucus.
And they won't understand its importance, it's too bad,
Not even when it's too late.

Now we're often happy. The dark car
Moves heftily away along low bluffs,
And if we don't have our feelings, what
Good are we, but whose business is it?
Beware the happy man: once she perched light
In the reading space of my room, a present joy
For all time to come, whatever happens;
And still we rotate, gathering speed until
Nothing is there but more speed in the light ahead.
Such moments as we prized in life:
The promise of a new day, living with lots of people
All headed in more or less the same direction, the sound of this
In the embracing stillness, but not the brutality,
And lists of examples of lots of things, and shit—
What more could we conceivably be satisfied with, it is
Joy, and undaunted
She leaves the earth at that point,

Intersecting all our daydreams of breakfast and lunch.
The Lady of Shalott's in hot water again.

This and the dreams of any of the young
Were not her care. The river flowed
Hard by the hospital from whose gilded
Balconies and turrets fair spirits waved,
Lonely, like us. Here be no pursuers,
Only imagined animals and cries
In the wilderness, which made it "the wilderness,"
And suddenly the lonesomeness becomes a pleasant city
Fanning out around a lake; you get to meet
Precisely the person who would have been here now,
A dream no longer, and are polished and directed
By his deliberate grasp, back
To the reality that was always there despairing
Of your return as months and years went by,
Now silent again forever, the perfect space,
Attuned to your wristwatch
As though time would never go away again.

His dirty mind
Produced it all, an oratorio based on love letters
About our sexual habits in the early 1950s.
It wasn't that these stories weren't true,
Only that a different kind of work
Of the imagination had grown up around them, taller
Than redwoods, and not
Wanting to embarrass them, effaced itself
To the extent that a colossus could, and so you looked
And saw nothing, but suddenly felt better
Without wondering why. And the serial continues:
Pain, expiation, delight, more pain,
A frieze that lengthens continually, in the happy way

Friezes do, and no plot is produced,
Nothing you could hang an identifying question on.
It's an imitation of pleasure; it may not work
But at least we'll know then that we'll have done
What we could, and chalk it up to virtue
Or just plain laziness. And if she glides
Backwards through us, a finger hooked
Out of death, we shall not know where the mystery began:
Inaccurate dreamers of our state,
Sodden from sitting in the rain too long.

· DESTINY WALTZ ·

Everyone has some work to be done
And after that they may have some fun.
Which sometimes leads to distraction.
Older faces than yours

Have been whirled away on heaven
Knows what wind like painted leaves in autumn.
Seriousness doesn't help either:
Just when you get on it it slips its tether,
Laughing, runs happily away.

It is a question of forbearance among the days.
Ask, but not too often: that way most ways
Of leading up to the truth will approach you
Timidly at first, wanting to get to know you
Before wandering away on other paths
Leading out of your meanwhile safe precinct.
Your feet know what they're doing.

And if later in the year some true fear,
A real demon comes to be installed
In the sang-froid of not doing anything,
The shoe is on the other foot
This time,
Just this one time.

Romance removes so much of this
Yet staying behind while it does so
Is no way to agitate
To break the year's commotion where it loomed
Sharpest and most full. It's a trance.

· TRY ME!
I'M DIFFERENT! ·

Obviously the guts and beauty are going to be denied again
This time around, as we all meet at twilight
In a level place surrounded by tall trees. It's another kind of contest.
Whatever is sworn, promised, sealed
With kisses, over and over, is as strange, faithless
And fundamentally unlike us as the ocean when it fills
Deep crevices far inland, more deeply involved with the land
Than anyone suspected. Such are our games,

And so also the way we thought of them
In the time behind the telling. Now it goes smoothly
Under glass. The contours and color contrasts are
Sharper, but there is no sound. And I didn't deliberately
Try to hide my ambition, wearing the same tweed jacket
For the fourteenth season; instead I thought its pedigree something
To notice. But the question of style has been
Turned inside out in the towns where we never meet.

I lived so long without being scolded that I grew
To feel I was beyond criticism, until I flew
Those few paces from the nest. Now, I understand,
My privilege means giving up all claims on life
As the casual, criminal thing it sometimes is, in favor of
A horizon in whose cursive recesses we
May sometimes lie concealed because we are part
Of the pattern. No one misses you. The future

Ignores those streaming with a present so heavy
And intense we are subdued by the outline.
No one criticizes us for lacking depth,
But the scandal shimmers, around and elsewhere.
If we could finally pry open the gate to the pastures of the times,
No sickness would be evident. And the colors we adduced
Would supply us, parables ourselves, told in our own words.

must never be *invented.* It shall have been.
Once its umbrella of truth is raised to become
And tall trees follow it as though it were Orpheus,
Its music, in trouble, slows down to a complete standstill,

Still in trouble but has become a cube
With all the outside faces reflecting
What we did before we got here. One of us,
A little poorer than the others, half-turns

To divulge a truth in low relief that another
Messenger would have been killed for: it isn't
Our waiting that makes us worthy of having been here forever,
Only the wild groves you read about, that no one

Has probably ever seen. I hear they have caves
In which men as old as the earth live, that when
These die, nothing ever takes their place.
Therefore, why weep we, mourners, around

A common block of space?

· WHATEVER IT IS,
WHEREVER YOU ARE ·

The cross-hatching technique which allowed our ancestors to exchange certain genetic traits for others, in order to provide their offspring with a way of life at once more variegated and more secure than their own, has just about run out of steam and has left us wondering, once more, what there is about this plush solitude that makes us think we will ever get out, or even want to. The ebony hands of the clock always seem to mark the same hour. That is why it always seems the same, though it is of course changing constantly, subtly, as though fed by an underground stream. If only we could go out in back, as when we were kids, and smoke and fool around and just stay out of the way, for a little while. But that's just it—don't you see? We are "out in back." No one has ever used the front door. We have always lived in this place without a name, without shame, a place for grownups to talk and laugh, having a good time. When we were children it seemed that adulthood would be like climbing a tree, that there would be a view from there, breathtaking because slightly more elusive. But now we can see only down, first down through the branches and further down the surprisingly steep grass patch that slopes away from the base of the tree. It certainly is a different view, but not the one we expected.

What did *they* want us to do? Stand around this way, monitoring every breath, checking each impulse for the return address, wondering constantly about evil until necessarily we fall into a state of torpor that is probably the worst sin of all? To what purpose did they cross-hatch so effectively, so that the luminous surface that was underneath is transformed into another, also luminous but so shifting and so alive with suggestiveness that it is like quicksand, to take a step there would be to fall through the fragile net of uncertainties into the bog of certainty, otherwise known as the Slough of Despond?

Probably they meant for us to enjoy the things they enjoyed, like late summer evenings, and hoped that we'd find others and thank them for providing us with the wherewithal to find and enjoy them. Singing the way they did, in the old time, we can sometimes see through the tissues and tracings the genetic process has laid down between us and them. The tendrils can suggest a hand, or a specific color—the yellow of the tulip, for instance—will flash for a moment in such a way that after it has been withdrawn we can be sure that there was no imagining, no auto-suggestion here, but at the same time it becomes as useless as all subtracted memories. It has brought certainty without heat or light. Yet still in the old time, in the faraway summer evenings, they must have had a word for this, or known that we would someday need one, and wished to help. Then it is that a kind of purring occurs, like the wind sneaking around the baseboards of a room: not the infamous "still, small voice" but an ancillary speech that is parallel to the slithering of our own doubt-fleshed imaginings, a visible soundtrack of the way we sound as we move from encouragement to despair to exasperation and back again, with a gesture sometimes that is like an aborted movement outward toward some cape or promontory from which the view would extend in two directions—backward and forward—but that is only a polite hope in the same vein as all the others, crumpled and put away, and almost not to be distinguished from any of them, except that *it knows we know*, and in the context of not knowing is a fluidity that flashes like silver, that seems to say a film has been exposed and an image will, most certainly will, not like the last time, come to consider itself within the frame.

It must be an old photograph of you, out in the yard, looking almost afraid in the crisp, raking light that afternoons in the city held in those days, unappeased, not accepting anything from anybody. So what else is new? I'll tell you what is: you are accepting this now from the invisible, unknown sender, and the light that was intended, you thought, only to rake or glance is now directed full in your face, as it in fact always was, but you were squinting so hard, fearful of accepting it, that you didn't know this. Whether it warms or burns is another matter, which we will not go into here. The point is that you are accepting it and holding on to it, like love from someone you always thought you couldn't stand, and whom you now recognize as a brother, an equal. Someone whose face is the same as yours in the photograph but who is someone else, all of whose thoughts and feelings are directed at you, falling like a gentle slab of light that will ultimately loosen and dissolve the crusted suspicion, the timely self-hatred, the efficient cold directness, the horrible good manners, the sensible resolves and the senseless nights spent waiting in utter abandon, that have grown up to be you in the tree with no view; and place you firmly in the good-natured circle of your ancestors' games and entertainments.

· TREFOIL ·

Imagine some tinkling curiosity from the years back—
The fashions aren't old enough yet to look out of fashion.
It is a picture of patient windows, with trees
Of two minds half-caught in their buzz and luster,
The froth of everyone's ideas as personal and skimpy as ever.

The windows taught us one thing: a great, square grief
Not alleviated or distracted by anything, since the pattern
Must establish itself before it can grow old, cannot weather nicely
Keeping a notion of squirrels and peacocks to punctuate
Chapters of fine print as they are ground down, growing ever finer
To assume the strict title of dust someday. No, there is no room now
For oceans, blizzards: only night, with fingers of steel
Pressing the lost lid, searching forever unquietly the mechanism
To unclasp all this into warbled sunlight, the day
The gaunt parson comes to ask for your hand. Nothing is flying,
Sinking; it is as though the resistance of all things
To the earth were so much casual embroidery, years
In the making, barely glimpsed at the appointed time.

Through it all a stiffness persists
Of someone who had changed her mind, moved by your arguments
And waiting till the last possible moment to confess it,
To let you know you were wanted, even a lot, more than you could
Imagine. But all that is, as they say, another story.

· PROBLEMS ·

Rough stares, sometimes a hello,
A something to carry. Yes and over it
The feeling of one to one like leaves blowing
Between this imaginary, real world and the sky
Which is sometimes a terrible color
But is surely always and only as we imagine it?
I forgot to say there are extra things.
Once, someone—my father—came to me and spoke
Extreme words amid the caution of the time.
I was too drunk, too scared to know what was being said
Around us then, only that it was a final
Shelving off, that it was now and never,
The way things would come to pass.
You can subscribe to this.
It always lets you know how well
You're doing, how well along the thing is with its growing.
Was it a pattern of wheat
On the spotted walls you wanted to show me
Or are these the things always coming,
The churning, moving support that lets us rock still?

· A WAVE ·

To pass through pain and not know it,
A car door slamming in the night.
To emerge on an invisible terrain.

So the luck of speaking out
A little too late came to be worshipped in various guises:
A mute actor, a future saint intoxicated with the idea of martyrdom;
And our landscape came to be as it is today:
Partially out of focus, some of it too near, the middle distance
A haven of serenity and unreachable, with all kinds of nice
People and plants waking and stretching, calling
Attention to themselves with every artifice of which the human
Genre is capable. And they called it our home.

No one came to take advantage of these early
Reverses, no doorbell rang;
Yet each day of the week, once it had arrived, seemed the threshold
Of love and desperation again. At night it sang
In the black trees: *My mindless, oh my mindless, oh.*
And it could be that it was Tuesday, with dark, restless clouds
And puffs of white smoke against them, and below, the wet streets
That seem so permanent, and all of a sudden the scene changes:
It's another idea, a new conception, something submitted
A long time ago, that only now seems about to work
To destroy at last the ancient network
Of letters, diaries, ads for civilization.
It passes through you, emerges on the other side
And is now a distant city, with all
The possibilities shrouded in a narrative moratorium.
The chroniqueurs who bad-mouthed it, the honest
Citizens whose going down into the day it was,
Are part of it, though none
Stand with you as you mope and thrash your way through time,

Imagining it as it is, a kind of tragic euphoria
In which your spirit sprouted. And which is justified in you.

In the haunted house no quarter is given: in that respect
It's very much business as usual. The reductive principle
Is no longer there, or isn't enforced as much as before.
There will be no getting away from the prospector's
Hunch; past experience matters again; the tale will stretch on
For miles before it is done. There would be more concerts
From now on, and the ground on which a man and his wife could
Look at each other and laugh, remembering how love is to them,
Shrank and promoted a surreal intimacy, like jazz music
Moving over furniture, to say how pleased it was
Or something. In the end only a handshake
Remains, something like a kiss, but fainter. Were we
Making sense? Well, that thirst will account for some
But not all of the marvelous graffiti; meanwhile
The oxygen of the days sketches the rest,
The balance. Our story is no longer alone.
There is a rumbling there
And now it ends, and in a luxurious hermitage
The straws of self-defeat are drawn. The short one wins.

One idea is enough to organize a life and project it
Into unusual but viable forms, but many ideas merely
Lead one thither into a morass of their own good intentions.
Think how many the average person has during the course of a day, or night,
So that they become a luminous backdrop to ever-repeated
Gestures, having no life of their own, but only echoing
The suspicions of their possessor. It's fun to scratch around
And maybe come up with something. But for the tender blur
Of the setting to mean something, words must be ejected bodily,
A certain crispness be avoided in favor of a density
Of strutted opinion doomed to wilt in oblivion: not too linear

Nor yet too puffed and remote. Then the advantage of
Sinking in oneself, crashing through the skylight of one's own
Received opinions redirects the maze, setting up significant
Erections of its own at chosen corners, like gibbets,
And through this the mesmerizing plan of the landscape becomes,
At last, apparent. It is no more a landscape than a golf course is,
Though sensibly a few natural bonuses have been left in. And as it
Focuses itself, it is the backward part of a life that is
Partially coming into view. It's there, like a limb. And the issue
Of making sense becomes such a far-off one. Isn't this "sense"—
This little of my life that I can see—that answers me
Like a dog, and wags its tail, though excitement and fidelity are
About all that ever gets expressed? What did I ever do
To want to wander over into something else, an explanation
Of how I behaved, for instance, when knowing can have this
Sublime rind of excitement, like the shore of a lake in the desert
Blazing with the sunset? So that if it pleases all my constructions
To collapse, I shall at least have had that satisfaction, and known
That it need not be permanent in order to stay alive,
Beaming, confounding with the spell of its good manners.

As with rocks at low tide, a mixed surface is revealed,
More detritus. Still, it is better this way
Than to have to live through a sequence of events acknowledged
In advance in order to get to a primitive statement. And the mind
Is the beach on which the rocks pop up, just a neutral
Support for them in their indignity. They explain
The trials of our age, cleansing it of toxic
Side-effects as it passes through their system.
Reality. Explained. And for seconds
We live in the same body, are a sibling again.

I think all games and disciplines are contained here,
Painting, as they go, dots and asterisks that

We force into meanings that don't concern us
And so leave us behind. But there are no fractions, the world is an integer
Like us, and like us it can neither stand wholly apart nor disappear.
When one is young it seems like a very strange and safe place,
But now that I have changed it feels merely odd, cold
And full of interest. The sofa that was once a seat
Puzzles no longer, while the sweet conversation that occurs
At regular intervals throughout the years is like a collie
One never outgrows. And it happens to you
In this room, it is here, and we can never
Eat of the experience. It drags us down. Much later on
You thought you perceived a purpose in the game at the moment
Another player broke one of the rules; it seemed
A module for the wind, something in which you lose yourself
And are not lost, and then it pleases you to play another day
When outside conditions have changed and only the game
Is fast, perplexed and true, as it comes to have seemed.

Yet one does know why. The covenant we entered
Bears down on us, some are ensnared, and the right way,
It turns out, is the one that goes straight through the house
And out the back. By so many systems
As we are involved in, by just so many
Are we set free on an ocean of language that comes to be
Part of us, as though we would ever get away.
The sky is bright and very wide, and the waves talk to us,
Preparing dreams we'll have to live with and use. The day will come
When we'll have to. But for now
They're useless, more trees in a landscape of trees.

I hadn't expected a glance to be that direct, coming from a sculpture
Of moments, thoughts added on. And I had kept it
Only as a reminder, not out of love. In time I moved on
To become its other side, and then, gentle, anxious, I became as a parent

To those scenes lifted from "real life." There was the quiet time
In the supermarket, and the pieces
Of other people's lives as they sashayed or tramped past
My own section of a corridor, not pausing
In many cases to wonder where they were—maybe they even knew.
True, those things or moments of which one
Finds oneself an enthusiast, a promoter, are few,
But they last well,
Yielding up their appearances for form
Much later than the others. Forgetting about "love"
For a moment puts one miles ahead, on the steppe or desert
Whose precise distance as it feels I
Want to emphasize and estimate. Because
We will all have to walk back this way
A second time, and not to know it then, not
To number each straggling piece of sagebrush
Is to sleep before evening, and well into the night
That always coaxes us out, smooths out our troubles and puts us back to bed
    again.

All those days had a dumb clarity that was about getting out
Into a remembered environment. The headlines and economy
Would refresh for a moment as you look back over the heap
Of rusted box-springs with water under them, and then,
Like sliding up to a door or a peephole a tremendous advantage
Would burst like a bubble. Toys as solemn and knotted as books
Assert themselves first, leading down through a delicate landscape
Of reminders to be better next time to a damp place on my hip,
And this would spell out a warm business letter urging us
All to return to our senses, to the matter of the day
That was ending now. And no special sense of decline ensued
But perhaps a few moments of music of such tact and weariness
That one awakens with a new sense of purpose: more things to be done
And the just-sufficient tools to begin doing them

While awaiting further orders that must materialize soon
Whether in the sand-pit with frightened chickens running around
Or on a large table in a house deep in the country with messages
Pinned to the walls and a sense of plainness quite unlike
Any other waiting. I am prepared to deal with this
While putting together notes related to the question of love
For the many, for two people at once, and for myself
In a time of need unlike those that have arisen so far.
And some day perhaps the discussion that has to come
In order for us to start feeling any of it before we even
Start to think about it will arrive in a new weather
Nobody can imagine but which will happen just as the ages
Have happened without causing total consternation,
Will take place in a night, long before sleep and the love
That comes then, breathing mystery back into all the sterile
Living that had to lead up to it. Moments as clear as water
Splashing on a rock in the sun, though in darkness, and then
Sleep has to affirm it and the body is fresh again,
For the trials and dangerous situations that any love,
However well-meaning, has to use as terms in the argument
That is the reflexive play of our living and being lost
And then changed again, a harmless fantasy that must grow
Progressively serious, and soon state its case succinctly
And dangerously, and we sit down to the table again
Noting the grain of the wood this time and how it pushes through
The pad we are writing on and becomes part of what is written.
Not until it starts to stink does the inevitable happen.

Moving on we approached the top
Of the thing, only it was dark and no one could see,
Only somebody said it was a miracle we had gotten past the
Previous phase, now faced with each other's conflicting
Wishes and the hope for a certain peace, so this would be
Our box and we would stay in it for as long

As we found it comfortable, for the broken desires
Inside were as nothing to the steeply shelving terrain outside,
And morning would arrange everything. So my first impulse
Came, stayed awhile, and left, leaving behind
Nothing of itself, no whisper. The days now move
From left to right and back across this stage and no one
Notices anything unusual. Meanwhile I have turned back
Into that dream of rubble that was the city of our starting out.
No one advises me; the great tenuous clouds of the desert
Sky visit it and they barely touch, so pleasing in the
Immense solitude are the tracks of those who wander and continue
On their route, certain that day will end soon and that night will then fall.

But behind what looks like heaps of slag the peril
Consists in explaining everything too evenly. Those
Suffering from the blahs are unlikely to notice that the topic
Of today's lecture doesn't exist yet, and in their trauma
Will become one with the vast praying audience as it sways and bends
To the rhythm of an almost inaudible piccolo. And when
It is flushed out, the object of all this meditation will not
Infrequently turn out to be a mere footnote to the great chain
That manages only with difficulty to connect earth and sky together.
Are comments like ours really needed? Of course, heaven is nice
About it, not saying anything, but we, when we come away
As children leaving school at four in the afternoon, can we
Hold our heads up and face the night's homework? No, the
Divine tolerance we seem to feel is actually in short supply,
And those moving forward toward us from the other end of the bridge
Are defending, not welcoming us to, the place of power,
A hill ringed with low, ridgelike fortifications. But when
Somebody better prepared crosses over, he or she will get the same
Cold reception. And so because it is impossible to believe
That anyone lives there, it is we who shall be homeless, outdoors

At the end. And we won't quite know what to do about it.
It's mind-boggling, actually. Each of us must try to concentrate
On some detail or other of their armor: somber, blood-red plumes
Floating over curved blue steel; the ribbed velvet stomacher
And its more social implications. Hurry to deal with the sting
Of added meaning, hurry to fend it off. Your lessons
Will become the ground of which we are made
And shall look back on, for awhile. Life was pleasant there.
And though we made it all up, it could still happen to us again.
Only then, watch out. The burden of proof of the implausible
Picaresque tale, boxes within boxes, will be yours
Next time round. And nobody is going to like your ending.

We had, though, a feeling of security
But we weren't aware of it then: that's
How secure we were. Now, in the dungeon of Better Living,
It seems we may be called back and interrogated about it
Which would be unfortunate, since only the absence of memory
Animates us as we walk briskly back and forth
At one with the soulless, restless crowd on the somber avenue.
Is there something new to see, to speculate on? Dunno, better
Stand back until something comes along to explain it,
This curious lack of anxiety that begins to gnaw
At one. Did it come because happiness hardened everything
In its fire, and so the forms cannot die, like a ruined
Fort too strong to be pulled down? And something like pale
Alpine flowers still flourishes there:
Some reminder that can never be anything more than that,
Yet its balm cares about something, we cannot be really naked
Having this explanation. So a reflected image of oneself
Manages to stay alive through the darkest times, a period
Of unprecedented frost, during which we get up each morning
And go about our business as usual.

. . .
And though there are some who leave regularly
For the patchwork landscape of childhood, north of here,
Our own kind of stiff standing around, waiting helplessly
And mechanically for instructions that never come, suits the space
Of our intense, uncommunicated speculation, marries
The still life of crushed, red fruit in the sky and tames it
For observation purposes. One is almost content
To be with people then, to read their names and summon
Greetings and speculation, or even nonsense syllables and
Diagrams from those who appear so brilliantly at ease
In the atmosphere we made by getting rid of most amenities
In the interests of a bare, strictly patterned life that apparently
Has charms we weren't even conscious of, which is
All to the good, except that it fumbles the premise
We put by, saving it for a later phase of intelligence, and now
We are living on it, ready to grow and make mistakes again,
Still standing on one leg while emerging continually
Into an inexpressive void, the blighted fields
Of a kiss, the rope of a random, unfortunate
Observation still around our necks though we thought we
Had cast it off in a novel that has somehow gotten stuck
To our lives, battening on us. A sad condition
To see us in, yet anybody
Will realize that he or she has made those same mistakes,
Memorized those same lists in the due course of the process
Being served on you now. Acres of bushes, treetops;
Orchards where the quince and apple seem to come and go
Mysteriously over long periods of time; waterfalls
And what they conceal, including what comes after—roads and roadways
Paved for the gently probing, transient automobile;
Farragoes of flowers; everything, in short,
That makes this explicit earth what it appears to be in our

Glassiest moments when a canoe shoots out from under some foliage
Into the river and finds it calm, not all that exciting but above all
Nothing to be afraid of, celebrates us
And what we have made of it.

Not something so very strange, but then seeming ordinary
Is strange too. Only the way we feel about the everything
And not the feeling itself is strange, strange to us, who live
And want to go on living under the same myopic stars we have known
Since childhood, when, looking out a window, we saw them
And immediately liked them.

And we can get back to that raw state
Of feeling, so long deemed
Inconsequential and therefore appropriate to our later musings
About religion, about migrations. What is restored
Becomes stronger than the loss as it is remembered;
Is a new, separate life of its own. A new color. Seriously blue.
Unquestioning. Acidly sweet. Must we then pick up the pieces
(But what are the pieces, if not separate puzzles themselves,
  And meanwhile rain abrades the window?) and move to a central clearing-
    house
Somewhere in Iowa, far from the distant bells and thunderclaps that
Make this environment pliant and distinct? Nobody
Asked me to stay here, at least if they did I forgot, but I can
Hear the dust at the pores of the wood, and know then
The possibility of something more liberated and gracious
Though not of this time. Failing
That there are the books we haven't read, and just beyond them
A landscape stippled by frequent glacial interventions
That holds so well to its lunette one wants to keep it but we must
Go on despising it until that day when environment
Finally reads as a necessary but still vindictive opposition

To all caring, all explaining. Your finger traces a
Bleeding violet line down the columns of an old directory and to this spongy
State of talking things out a glass exclamation point opposes
A discrete claim: forewarned. So the voluminous past
Accepts, recycles our claims to present consideration
And the urban landscape is once again untroubled, smooth
As wax. As soon as the oddity is flushed out
It becomes monumental and anxious once again, looking
Down on our lives as from a baroque pinnacle and not the
Mosquito that was here twenty minutes ago.
The past absconds
With our fortunes just as we were rounding a major
Bend in the swollen river; not to see ahead
Becomes the only predicament when what
Might be sunken there is mentioned only
In crabbed allusions but will be back tomorrow.

It takes only a minute revision, and see—the thing
Is there in all its interested variegatedness,
With prospects and walks curling away, never to be followed,
A civilized concern, a never being alone.
Later on you'll have doubts about how it
Actually was, and certain greetings will remain totally forgotten,
As water forgets a dam once it's over it. But at this moment
A spirit of independence reigns. Quietude
To get out and do things in, and a rush back to the house
When evening turns up, and not a moment too soon.
Headhunters and jackals mingle with the viburnum
And hollyhocks outside, and it all adds up, pointedly,
To something one didn't quite admit feeling uneasy about, but now
That it's all out in the open, like a successful fire
Burning in a fireplace, really there's no cause for alarm.
For even when hours and days go by in silence and the phone

Never rings, and widely spaced drops of water
Fall from the eaves, nothing is any longer a secret
And one can live alone rejoicing in this:
That the years of war are far off in the past or the future,
That memory contains everything. And you see slipping down a hallway
The past self you decided not to have anything to do with any more
And it is a more comfortable you, dishonest perhaps,
But alive. Wanting you to know what you're losing.
And still the machinery of the great exegesis is only beginning
To groan and hum. There are moments like this one
That are almost silent, so that bird-watchers like us
Can come, and stay awhile, reflecting on shades of difference
In past performances, and move on refreshed.

But always and sometimes questioning the old modes
And the new wondering, the poem, growing up through the floor,
Standing tall in tubers, invading and smashing the ritual
Parlor, demands to be met on its own terms now,
Now that the preliminary negotiations are at last over.
You could be lying on the floor,
Or not have time for too much of any one thing,
Yet you know the song quickens in the bones
Of your neck, in your heel, and there is no point
In looking out over the yard where tractors run,
The empty space in the endless continuum
Of time has come up: the space that can be filled only by you.
And I had thought about the roadblocks, wondered
Why they were less frequent, wondered what progress the blizzard
Might have been making a certain distance back there,
But it was not enough to save me from choosing
Myself now, from being the place I have to get to
Before nightfall and under the shelter of trees
It is true but also without knowing out there in the dark,

Being alone at the center of a moan that did not issue from me
And is pulling me back toward old forms of address
I know I have already lived through, but they are strong again,
And big to fill the exotic spaces that arguing left.

So all the slightly more than young
Get moved up whether they like it or not, and only
The very old or the very young have any say in the matter,
Whether they are a train or a boat or just a road leading
Across a plain, from nowhere to nowhere. Later on
A record of the many voices of the middle-young will be issued
And found to be surprisingly original. That can't concern us,
However, because now there isn't space enough,
Not enough dimension to guarantee any kind of encounter
The stage-set it requires at the very least in order to burrow
Profitably through history and come out having something to say,
Even just one word with a slightly different intonation
To cause it to stand out from the backing of neatly invented
Chronicles of things men have said and done, like an English horn,
And then to sigh, to faint back
Into all our imaginings, dark
And viewless as they are,
Windows painted over with black paint but
We can sufficiently imagine, so much is admitted, what
Might be going on out there and even play some part
In the ordering of it all into lengths of final night,
Of dim play, of love that at lasts oozes through the seams
In the cement, suppurates, subsumes
All the other business of living and dying, the orderly
Ceremonials and handling of estates,
Checking what does not appear normal and drawing together
All the rest into the report that will finally be made
On a day when it does not appear that there is anything to receive it
Properly and we wonder whether we too are gone,

Buried in our love,
The love that defined us only for a little while,
And when it strolls back a few paces, to get another view,
Fears that it may have encountered eternity in the meantime.
And as the luckless describe love in glowing terms to strangers
In taverns, and the seemingly blessed may be unaware of having lost it,
So always there is a small remnant
Whose lives are congruent with their souls
And who ever afterward know no mystery in it,
The cimmerian moment in which all lives, all destinies
And incompleted destinies were swamped
As though by a giant wave that picks itself up
Out of a calm sea and retreats again into nowhere
Once its damage is done.
And what to say about those series
Of infrequent pellucid moments in which
One reads inscribed as though upon an empty page
The strangeness of all those contacts from the time they erupt
Soundlessly on the horizon and in a moment are upon you
Like a stranger on a snowmobile
But of which nothing can be known or written, only
That they passed this way? That to be bound over
To love in the dark, like Psyche, will somehow
Fill the sheaves of pages with a spidery, Spencerian hand
When all that will be necessary will be to go away
For a few minutes in order to return and find the work completed?
And so it is the only way
That love determines us, and we look the same
To others when they happen in afterwards, and cannot even know
We have changed, so massive in our difference
We are, like a new day that looks and cannot be the same
As those we used to reckon with, and so start
On our inane rounds again too dumb to profit from past
Mistakes—that's how different we are!

. . .

But once we have finished being interrupted
There is no longer any population to tell us how the gods
Had wanted it—only—so the story runs—a vast forest
With almost nobody in it. Your wants
Are still halfheartedly administered to; sometimes there is milk
And sometimes not, but a ladder of hilarious applause
No longer leads up to it. Instead, there's that cement barrier.
The forest ranger was nice, but warning us away,
Reminded you how other worlds can as easily take root
Like dandelions, in no time. There's no one here now
But émigrés, with abandoned skills, so near
To the surface of the water you can touch them through it.
It's they can tell you how love came and went
And how it keeps coming and going, ever disconcerting,
Even through the topiary trash of the present,
Its undoing, and smiles and seems to recognize no one.
It's all attitudinizing, maybe, images reflected off
Some mirrored surface we cannot see, and they seem both solid
As a suburban home and graceful phantasms, at ease
In any testing climate you may contrive. But surely
The slightly sunken memory that remains, accretes, is proof
That there were doings, yet no one admits to having heard
Even of these. You pass through lawns on the way to it; it's late
Even though the light is strongly yellow; and are heard
Commenting on how hard it is to get anybody to do anything
Any more; suddenly your name is remembered at the end—
It's there, on the list, was there all along
But now is too defunct to cope
Which may be better in the long run: we'll hear of
Other names, and know we don't want them, but that love
Was somehow given out to one of them by mistake,
Not utterly lost. Boyish, slipping past high school
Into the early forties, disingenuous though, yet all

The buds of this early spring won't open, which is surprising,
He says. It isn't likely to get any warmer than it is now.
In today's mainstream one mistakes him, sincerely, for someone else;
He passed on slowly and turns a corner. One can't say
He was gone before you knew it, yet something of that, some tepid
Challenge that was never taken up and disappeared forever,
Surrounds him. Love is after all for the privileged.

But there is something else—call it a consistent eventfulness,
A common appreciation of the way things have of enfolding
When your attention is distracted for a moment, and then
It's all bumps and history, as though this crusted surface
Had always been around, didn't just happen to come into being
A short time ago. The scarred afternoon is unfortunate
Perhaps, but as they come to see each other dimly
And for the first time, an internal romance
Of the situation rises in these human beings like sap
And they can at last know the fun of not having it all but
Having instead a keen appreciation of the ways in which it
Underachieves as well as rages: an appetite,
For want of a better word. In darkness and silence.

In the wind, it is living. What were the interruptions that
Led us here and then shanghaied us if not sincere attempts to
Understand and so desire another person, it doesn't
Matter which one, and then, self-abandoned, to build ourselves
So as to desire him fully, and at the last moment be
Taken aback at such luck: the feeling, invisible but alert.
On that clear February evening thirty-three years ago it seemed
A tapestry of living sounds shading to colors, and today
On this brick stump of an office building the colors are shaggy
Again, are at last what they once were, proving
They haven't changed: you have done that,
Not they. All that remains is to get to know them,

Like a twin brother from whom you were separated at birth
For whom the factory sounds now resonate in an uplifting
Sunset of your own choosing and fabrication, a rousing
Anthem to perpendicularity and the perennial exponential
Narration to cause everything to happen by evoking it
Within the framework of shared boredom and shared responsibilities.
Cheerful ads told us it was all going to be OK,
That the superstitions would do it all for you. But today
It's bigger and looser. People are not out to get you
And yet the walkways look dangerous. The smile slowly soured.
Still, coming home through all this
And realizing its vastness does add something to its dimension:
Teachers would never have stood for this. Which is why
Being tall and shy, you can still stand up more clearly
To the definition of what you are. You are not a sadist
But must only trust in the dismantling of that definition
Some day when names are being removed from things, when all attributes
Are sinking in the maelstrom of de-definition like spars.
You must then come up with something to say,
Anything, as long as it's no more than five minutes long,
And in the interval you shall have been washed. It's that easy.
But meanwhile, I know, stone tenements are still hoarding
The shadow that is mine; there is nothing to admit to,
No one to confess to. This period goes on for quite a few years
But as though along a low fence by a sidewalk. Then brandishes
New definitions in its fists, but these are evidently false
And get thrown out of court. Next you're on your own
In an old film about two guys walking across the United States.
The love that comes after will be richly satisfying,
Like rain on the desert, calling unimaginable diplomacy into being
Until you thought you should get off here, maybe this stop
Was yours. And then it all happens blindingly, over and over
In a continuous, vivid present that wasn't there before.
No need to make up stories at this juncture, everybody

Likes a joke and they find yours funny. And then it's just
Two giant steps down to the big needing and feeling
That is yours to grow in. Not grow old, the
Magic present still insists on being itself,
But to play in. To live and be lived by
And in this way bring all things to the sensible conclusion
Dreamed into their beginnings, and so arrive at the end.

Simultaneously in an area the size of West Virginia
The opposing view is climbing toward heaven: how swiftly
It rises! How slender the packed silver mass spiraling
Into further thinness, into what can only be called excess,
It seems, now. And anyway it sounds better in translation
Which is the only language you will read it in:
"I was lost, but seemed to be coming home,
Through quincunxes of apple trees, but ever
As I drew closer, as in Zeno's paradox, the mirage
Of home withdrew and regrouped a little farther off.
I could see white curtains fluttering at the windows
And in the garden under a big brass-tinted apple tree
The old man had removed his hat and was gazing at the grass
As though in sorrow, sorrow for what I had done.
Realizing it was now or never, I lurched
With one supreme last effort out of the dream
Onto the couch-grass behind the little red-painted palings:
I was here! But it all seemed so lonesome. I was welcomed
Without enthusiasm. My room had been kept as it was
But the windows were closed, there was a smell of a closed room.
And though I have been free ever since
To browse at will through my appetites, lingering
Over one that seemed special, the lamplight
Can never replace the sad light of early morning
Of the day I left, convinced (as indeed I am today)
Of the logic of my search, yet all unprepared

To look into the practical aspects, the whys and wherefores,
And so never know, eventually, whether I have accomplished
My end, or merely returned, another leaf that falls."
One must be firm not to be taken in by the histrionics
And even more by the rigorous logic with which the enemy
Deploys his message like iron trenches under ground
That rise here and there in blunt, undulating shapes.
And once you have told someone that none of it frightens you
There is still the breached sense of your own being
To live with, to somehow nurse back to plenitude:
Yet it never again has that hidden abundance,
That relaxed, joyous well-being with which
In other times it frolicked along roads, making
The best of ignorance and unconscious, innocent selfishness,
The spirit that was to occupy those times
Now transposed, sunk too deep in its own reflection
For memory. The eager calm of every day.
But in the end the dark stuff, the odd quick attack
Followed by periods of silence that get shorter and shorter
Resolves the subjective-versus-objective approach by undoing
The complications of our planet, its climate, its sonatinas
And stories, its patches of hard ugly snow waiting around
For spring to melt them. And it keeps some memories of the troubled
Beginning-to-be-resolved period even in the timely first inkling
Of maturity in March, "when night and day grow equal," but even
More in the solemn peach-harvest that happens some months later
After differing periods of goofing-off and explosive laughter.
To be always articulating these preludes, there seems to be no
Sense in it, if it is going to be perpetually five o'clock
With the colors of the bricks seeping more and more bloodlike through
    the tan
Of trees, and then only to blacken. But it says more
About us. When they finally come
With much laborious jangling of keys to unlock your cell

You can tell them yourself what it is,
Who you are, and how you happened to turn out this way,
And how they made you, for better or for worse, what you are now,
And how you seem to be, neither humble nor proud, *frei aber einsam.*

And should anyone question the viability of this process
You can point to the accessible result. Not like a great victory
That tirelessly sweeps over mankind again and again at the end
Of each era, presuming you can locate it, for the greater good
Of history, though you are not the first person to confuse
Its solicitation with something like scorn, but the slow polishing
Of an infinitely tiny cage big enough to hold all the dispiritedness,
Contempt, and incorrect conclusions based on false premises that now
Slow you down but by that time, enchaliced, will sound attentive,
Tonic even, an antidote to badly reasoned desiring: footfalls
Of the police approaching gingerly through the soft spring air.

At Pine Creek imitation the sky was no nearer. The difference
Was microtones, a seasoning between living and gestures.
It emerged as a rather stiff impression
Of all things. Not that there aren't those glad to have
A useful record like this to add to the collection
In the portfolio. But beyond just needing where is the need
To carry heaven around in one's breast-pocket? To satisfy
The hunger of millions with something more substantial than good wishes
And still withhold the final reassurance? So you see these
Days each with its disarming set of images and attitudes
Are beneficial perhaps but only after the last one
In every series has disappeared, down the road, forever, at night.

It would be cockier to ask of heaven just what is this present
Of an old dishpan you bestowed on me? Can I get out the door
With it, now that so many old enmities and flirtations have shrunk
To little more than fine print in the contexts of lives and so much
New ground is coming undone, shaken out like a scarf or a handkerchief

From this window that dominates everything perhaps a little too much?
In falling we should note the protective rush of air past us
And then pray for some day after the war to cull each of
The limited set of reflections we were given at the beginning
To try to make a fortune out of. Only then will some kind of radical stance
Have had some meaning, and for itself, not for us who lie gasping
On slopes never having had the nerve to trust just us, to go out with us
Not fearing some solemn overseer in the breath from the treetops.

And that that game-plan and the love we have been given for nothing
In particular should coincide—no, it is not yet time to think these things.
In vain would one try to peel off that love from the object it fits
So nicely, now, remembering it will have to be some day. You
Might as well offer it to your neighbor, the first one you meet, or throw
It away entirely, as plan to unlock on such and such a date
The door to this forest that has been your total upbringing.
No one expects it, and thus
Flares are launched out over the late disturbed landscape
Of items written down only to be forgotten once more, forever this time.

And already the sky is getting to be less salmon-colored,
The black clouds more meaningless (otter-shaped at first;
Now, as they retreat into incertitude, mere fins)
And perhaps it's too late for anything like the overhaul
That seemed called for, earlier, but whose initiative
Was it after all? I mean I don't mind staying here
A little longer, sitting quietly under a tree, if all this
Is going to clear up by itself anyway.

There is no indication this will happen,
But I don't mind. I feel at peace with the parts of myself
That questioned this other, easygoing side, chafed it
To a knotted rope of guesswork looming out of storms
And darkness and proceeding on its way into nowhere

Barely muttering. Always, a few errands
Summon us periodically from the room of our forethought
And that is a good thing. And such attentiveness
Besides! Almost more than anybody could bring to anything,
But we managed it, and with a good grace, too. Nobody
Is going to hold *that* against us. But since you bring up the question
I will say I am not unhappy to place myself entirely
At your disposal temporarily. Much that had drained out of living
Returns, in those moments, mounting the little capillaries
Of polite questions and seeming concern. I want it back.

And though that other question that I asked and can't
Remember any more is going to move still farther upward, casting
Its shadow enormously over where I remain, I can't see it.
Enough to know that I shall have answered for myself soon,
Be led away for further questioning and later returned
To the amazingly quiet room in which all my life has been spent.
It comes and goes; the walls, like veils, are never the same,
Yet the thirst remains identical, always to be entertained
And marveled at. And it is finally we who break it off,
Speed the departing guest, lest any question remain
Unasked, and thereby unanswered. Please, it almost
Seems to say, take me with you, I'm old enough. Exactly.
And so each of us has to remain alone, conscious of each other
Until the day when war absolves us of our differences. We'll
Stay in touch. So they have it, all the time. But all was strange.